ASH & BONE

A Novel

D1714090

Stephen A. White

1

Also by Stephen A. White
Available on Amazon
Time Passages
American Pop
Ersillia: Love & Loss
The Voice of Rage & Ruin
Murder at 33 RPM: A Rock 'n Roll Horror Story
A Slash in Time
With Sticks and Stones (and Frank X. Roberts)
Breaking Evil

On Air: My 50-Year Love Affair with Radio (with Jordan Rich)
Love Between the Pages (with Connie Thamert)
Front Row Center: How I Met Everyone (with Allan Dines)
The Magic of the Team (with Jim Hebert)

Visit Stephen A. White's Amazon Page

The sonnet at the end of this tale of guilt, betrayal and murder by arson, have been composed especially for the novel by my friend and occasional collaborator, the American poet Frank X. Roberts. Frank also penned the sonnet/curse used in my previous novel, *Breaking Evil,* about a spate of mysterious deaths during Boston's "Big Dig."

"When I get up at night I think about it. I shudder and try to brush it aside, just like you'd like to close the darkness out."

-- Frank H. Shapiro

Cocoanut Grove Survivor

Chapter One

Boston, MA ... November 28, 1942

"C'mon Mulvaney, move your fat Mick ass! This place is gonna be packed tonight!"

Seventeen-year-old Liam Mulvaney had been working at the Cocoanut Grove for nearly a year and he was used to the snide remarks from the club's owner, Mickey Alpert. Even though in 1942 Boston had an Irish Mayor—the Honorable Maurice Tobin—Liam knew that the Irish were still looked down upon, even in a city where they often dominated. Besides, he loved working at Boston's hottest night spot.

The Cocoanut Grove was a rather non-descript two-story brick building located at the corners of Piedmont Street and Shawmut Street. It boasted a main floor with a large dance area and huge 48-foot bar, with a smaller club/bar in the basement. You could get dinner on either floor, if you were willing to cough up $2 for a full dinner and fifty-cents for drinks. And most people were willing to do so as the club seemed to cater to the rich and famous, politicians and movie stars. Liam smiled as he remembered last summer seeing Rudy Vallee, Guy Lombardo, Sally Rand, and even Jimmy Durante hosting a table full of admirers as the champagne flowed like water while the club's maitre d', Angelo Lippi, kept everyone happy. Liam liked Angelo, who was always friendly to him, perhaps because the Italians weren't considered that much higher on the social scale than the Irish by the Boston bluebloods.

His boss might be a jerk, but he was right about one thing; the place was going to be packed this Saturday after Thanksgiving. Normally the club held about 500 people, but Liam could tell by the way he was scurrying about setting up tables, even on parts of the dance floor, that they were easily expecting at least a thousand patrons, including cowboy movie star Buck Jones, who Liam had seen on the screen in such classics as *Ghost Town* and *Forbidden Trail*. And Liam also knew there would be a large contingent of soldiers and sailors, many hoping for a last dance with a pretty girl and the chance to get their wick dipped before shipping off to fight in the Pacific.

As Liam went into a storeroom to grab some more folding chairs, he looked at an exit door that had been padlocked, something he never felt good about. Several of the club's exit doors were locked as a deterrent from having guests sneak out without paying their check. He frowned but went about his business. It was only 8 p.m. and already the club was filling up.

Just a little before 9 p.m., an exhausted Liam Mulvaney sat on a wooden box in a storeroom next to a door leading out to an alley off Shawmut Street. He normally worked until 10 p.m., but arranged to leave an hour earlier ("My mom's not feeling well.") so he'd be long gone when Conor came by. Liam leaned his head against the wall and closed his eyes, only to jump up when he heard someone enter the storage room, fearing it was his boss. That person, equally startled because she thought the room would be empty, was Peggy Regan, a beautiful 17-year old colleen who worked as a hat check girl upstairs. She was tall for a girl—at five feet, ten inches just a little shorter than he— and she had a beautiful face that was adorned with a wonderful scattering of freckles. But what Liam was always charmed by was that Peggy had the brightest red hair he had ever seen, which tonight was tied atop her head with a green ribbon. Since he had first seen her he had tried to muster the courage to ask her out.

"Oh, Liam... I didn't see you there," she said, flashing a beautiful smile. "Mr. Shea sent me down to grab a few bottles." Mr. Shea was the club's imposing bartender; William "Tiny" Shea, who tipped the scales north of 385 pounds. "Getting ready to go home?" she asked.

Liam sat back down. "Yeah, just catching my breath before heading out. How about you?"

Peggy frowned. "Sadly, here until midnight."

As she turned her attention back to the shelves, Liam finally felt some of his courage bubbling to the surface. He took a breath.

"Peggy, I was wondering..."

She turned to look at him. "Yes?"

"Well, I... I was... maybe..."

"Go out on a date?" she said, flashing a smile.

Dumbfounded, all Liam could do was nod.

"Sounds like fun. Maybe we can discuss it more tomorrow... I have to get these bottles upstairs." And with that she blew him a kiss and walked out of the room.

Sitting on the box, Liam couldn't believe how the day was turning out. And the opportunity to go on a date with Peggy Regan wasn't even the most remarkable thing that had happened.

Growing up in South Boston, Liam, like everyone else, knew who Danny "Fitzy" Fitzroy was. And what you knew was that you never crossed him, because Fitzroy controlled everything that went in and out of this part of the city, including liquor, gambling, even whispers of prostitution; it all followed Fitzroy around like a bad odor. He was mean and he was prone to acts of disturbing violence. Many an enemy of "Fitzy" Fitzroy could likely be found buried in the muck under a bridge somewhere in Boston.

Liam had never actually met Fitzroy, so he was surprised when a large man in a scalley cap approached him as he was walking down the street earlier that day and told him Mr.

Fitzroy wanted to talk with him. Not having the courage to ask why, Liam simply said "Okay," and the man led him to a small café on West Broadway. When he entered, he saw Fitzroy sitting in a booth. He knew him right away because Fitzroy was built like a fire-plug, with broad shoulders and a bullet shaped head. Liam also recognized the young man sitting beside him as Fitzroy's son, Conor, who was two years older than Liam. Conor was just the opposite of his father. He was tall and built like a linebacker, with tufts of brown hair that stuck out at odd angles, beady eyes, and a face that seemed carved into a permanent sneer. He was a bully and he was mean. One morning Liam had been walking through a park across from M Street when he saw Conor kick a dog to death simply because it had the nerve to bark at him. Liam never forgot the image of the dog's broken body lying on its side, letting out a last whimper before Conor smiled and walked away twirling a yo-yo.

Fitzroy waved him over, and Liam slowly approached while thinking in his head, "I am going to die, and I don't know why." Fitzroy attempted a smile (and failed) and motioned him to sit down. Liam did as he was told; his hands clenched nervously in his lap as Conor stared at him like a man on a diet eyeing a hot fudge sundae.

"You live over on East Seventh Street, with your mom, that right?" Fitzroy asked.

"Yes, sir."

"And my son tells me you work at the Cocoanut Grove?"

Liam wasn't sure how the gangster knew all this, but he wasn't about to ask. He simply nodded.

"How much they pay you over there?"

"I make $2.47, plus some tips."

Fitzroy nodded, and looking up Liam saw him glance over at his son, who was still smiling while his hand played with a steak knife, which Liam was pretty sure Conor Fitzroy would love to stick in his throat. Liam gulped.

"Now, that hardly seems like enough to take care of your ma, now does it?" Fitzroy said.

Liam wasn't sure how to answer, so he didn't. Fitzroy continued. "Tell you what, how would you like to make a hundred dollars?"

Liam wasn't sure he heard correctly; a hundred dollars? But Fitzroy confirmed it by saying, "And all you have to do is a little favor for us, something which I would really.... *really* appreciate."

"I don't understand," was all Liam could think to say. If Fitzroy was getting impatient, he wasn't showing it.

"You see, son, me and some of my associates will be conducting business at a bank tonight, and our meeting would go a lot smoother if there was a reason for the cops not to be in our general vicinity."

Liam was smart enough to know that banks weren't open on a Saturday night, so the rest of the story was pretty obvious.

"What do you want me to do?" Liam asked, still thinking about what he could do with $100.

Fitzroy sat back and lit a fat cigar. After he blew out a big puff of smoke he leaned forward on the table, his face no more than a few feet from Liam, who felt a bead of sweat make its way down his back.

"Nothing big. I figure tonight there's going to be some serious partying at the club, lots of people, dignitaries, famous people, like that," Fitzroy said. "So we need to create a small... disturbance, something that will pull all the cops in the city to the Cocoanut Grove sometime around 10 p.m."

"What kind of disturbance?"

Fitzroy waved the question away with a beefy hand. "Of no concern to you; Conor will take care of everything. All I need you to do is open up the back door off the Shawmut Street alley at 9 p.m. for him and go home. Easey-peazey." Fitzroy smiled and leaned back again and puffed away. But when he once again leaned forward the smile was gone and his eyes darkened. "And I'm sure it goes without saying that it would be in the best interest of both you and your dear old ma not to have a 'come-to-Jesus' moment, and that you understand this conversation *never happened.* Are we in agreement?"

Liam nodded as Conor slipped a $100 bill across the table. His lip turned into a sneer as he eyed Liam. "In that case, boyo," Conor said. "I'll see you at 9 p.m. sharp."

True to his word, at 9 p.m. there was a rap at the metal door and Liam leaped to his feet. He quickly unlocked the door and stepped aside as Conor walked in wearing a black leather coat. He patted Liam on the cheek. "Good lad," he said. "Now get the fuck out of here; I got work to do." He pushed Liam out into the alley and slammed the door shut. Liam stood there for a moment, thinking about what was going to happen. But the money in his pocket dissolved those thoughts and was replaced by a hunger caused by not eating all day. He decided instead of going right home to hit Klein's Deli around the corner for a pastrami sandwich and a shake.

On a Saturday night Klein's was packed and it wasn't until a few minutes before 10 p.m. that Liam finally got a table near the window facing Berkeley Street and ordered his meal. Ten minutes later a bored-looking waitress brought his food and Liam glanced briefly at a fire engine roaring by, its lights and siren blasting. Liam didn't give it much thought as he bit into his sandwich; after all it was Boston on a Saturday night.

The first real indication that something was terribly wrong happened a few minutes later when two police cars and another fire engine flew by his window, as patrons started to look out the door of the deli. Liam started to take another bite then froze when he heard the waitress yell, "The Cocoanut Grove is on fire!"

Running to the door, Liam pushed aside several people and stood on the sidewalk as another police car raced down the street towards the flames that were lapping at the sky a few blocks away. As he ran toward the club, he could see people racing in his direction, many coughing and gasping for air, several with faces blackened with soot. When he took the corner facing the club, he felt like his knees were buckling. What he saw was unimaginable.

Walking slowly towards the club, like a man in a daze, Liam could see flames coming from every opening in the building, as well as thick black smoke that blotted out what had once been a star-filled moonlit sky. There was chaos all around him as people screamed and either stumbled away or fell to the sidewalk. Liam saw several club patrons trying to administer assistance to those on the ground, but it seemed to no avail.

Liam's brain repelled against the smell of burned flesh. Husbands screamed for wives, wives screamed for husbands, the dying screamed in pain. Several soldiers and sailors tried to dislodge bodies that had piled up inside the revolving doors, as Liam sadly remembered that the management had chained many of the doors closed. A woman with her hair on fire stumbled past him, screaming out a name Liam couldn't understand.

Then Liam saw that off to the side lay a row of bodies covered in white sheets, obviously victims to the fire, smoke and super-heated air capable of turning a trachea and lungs to ash. Liam walked over to one of the bodies that had somehow caught his attention. He then fell to his knees and felt himself crying as he tried not to look at the red hair and green ribbon sticking out from beneath the soot-covered sheet.

That night, Liam Mulvaney's life changed forever.

Chapter Two

Boston, MA ... June 18, 1972

BOSTON HERALD TRAVELER
AND
Record American
PARTLY CLOUDY · LATE CITY · Complete

THE WEATHER: RAIN or DRIZZLE LIKELY (PAGE 38) · MONDAY, JUNE 19, 1972 · 44 PAGES · 426-3000 · FIFTEEN CENTS

A Message From the Publisher

9 Brave Men Honored

City Mourns Firefighters

CARROLL · HANBURY · DOLAN · JAMESON · BECKWITH · McGEE · BANLIS · MURPHY · BOUCHER

Son's 'Special Gift' Never Reached Dad

Heroes' Funerals On Thursday

"Good Lord."

That was all Liam Mulvaney could think to say as he stared up at the charred ruins of the Hotel Vendome, a once luxury hotel that was built 100 years ago at the corner of Commonwealth Avenue and Dartmouth Street in Boston's Back Bay.

It was a warm Sunday morning in June and Liam's view was of the back of the building while standing in Public Alley 424. Wisps of smoke still lingered from what steel and brick remained standing. Now four years as a Fire Investigator for the Massachusetts State Police, Liam had seen his share of fires, but this one was special... and not in a good way.

"It was a lot worse than it looks, Liam."

Liam was unaware that Deputy Chief Chuck O'Hara had come up beside him. He turned to look at his friend. "We lost nine good men yesterday," O'Hara said, and then suddenly he turned away. When he looked back he asked, "Did you know any of them?"

"Joey Saniuk. We graduated the Academy together in '56, day before St. Patty's. Celebrated together at Amrheins."

"Saniuk was a good man," O'Hara said.

"They were all good men, Chief,"

"Aye, that they were."

"So what happened?" Liam asked.

O'Hara composed himself, took a deep breath, and recounted the events that unfolded yesterday.

"From what I understand, the hotel was being converted into a combination condominium and office building. One of the construction guys saw a fire start between the third and fourth floors and gave us a call. We sent out 16 engine companies, five ladder companies, two aerial towers, and a heavy rescue company. We didn't want this one to get away from us."

"Makes sense," Liam agreed.

"Engine 33 and Ladder 15 responded first from their firehouse on Boylston Street near the Prudential Center, since they were the closest. Ladder 15 turned into Public Alley 424 at the rear of the hotel, where we are now, and raised its aerial to the fourth floor where they ran into a lot of heavy smoke. Engine 33 went to the front of the building."

"So far so good."

"That's what we thought," O'Hara said as sadness singed his voice. "But we were wrong. We were so very wrong."

"Go on."

19

O'Hara let out a long sigh. "Laddie, we took a heavy beating at the Vendome; a lot of fire, heavy smoke, and when the rake men were opening up we had to keep moving the line to kill the fire. And at one point we thought we had it licked. After about three hours we had the heavy fire knocked down and began looking for hidden fires."

"They can be trouble," Liam said.

"Tell me about it," O'Hara agreed. "Some of the men were rotating and taking a breather while the boys in Engine 37 were operating on the fourth floor when..."

Liam put his hand on O'Hara's heaving shoulders.

"...when the entire back section of the building, five floors, just fell. There was no warning, Liam. Down it went. One minute it was there and the next minute it wasn't. Ladder 15 was buried by the collapse; wrecked. Engine 7 was covered with plaster, dust, and smoke. It was chaos as everyone jumped in to save their friends. We had to remove the injured and recover the dead. Nine brothers died."

Liam looked up at the building once more. "Has there been a determination of the cause of the fire and the subsequent collapse?"

O'Hara shrugged, took out a handkerchief and blew his nose.

"They're saying when major alterations on the first floor of the structure were undertaken in the 1890's, a load-bearing wall was removed and cast-iron columns added, leaving just a seven-inch column as a main support above the second floor."

Liam let out a soft whistle. "Damn."

O'Hara continued. "Tell me about it. Add to that intense heat and about a million gallons of water and you have a recipe for disaster... which we never saw coming."

"I could see how that might happen," Liam said. "And the cause of the fire?"

"To be determined... which is why I guess you're here."

Liam nodded. "That's the plan."

O'Hara slapped Liam on the back. "In that case I'll let you get to work."

"Thanks."

O'Hara turned to go, and then stopped. "Oh, services are at the Cathedral of the Holy Cross tomorrow; Cardinal Medeiros doing the honors... I'll see you there?"

"Of course," Liam said, still looking up at the building.

Five minutes had passed since O'Hara departed, and Liam continued to stare up at the building, thinking about what he would be looking for when he went inside and also the nine firefighters that had perished in the worst fire in Boston since... 1942. And with that thought still lingering in his mind, Liam Mulvaney subconsciously touched his right knee, just at the spot where living tissue meets cold fiberglass... *and he remembered back almost eight years ago to the day.*

* * * * *

On Friday, May 22, 1964 it was a typical late spring day in Boston; 80-degrees, dry, but fairly windy. At just age 37, Liam was one of the youngest Fire Lieutenants with the Boston Fire Department, and his current command was a station house on Southampton Street, near Uphams Corner. It was 1:30 p.m. and Liam was getting more and more frustrated while fiddling with the radio dials, trying to pull in a rare Friday afternoon Red Sox game. The Red Sox were terrible last year, but the left-fielder Carl Yastrzemski had a excellent season and this year's prime rookie—Tony Conigliaro—even hit a home run last month in his first Fenway Park plate appearance. Hope springs eternal.

But then the station alarm clanged with reports of a house fire on Bellflower Street, which ran from Dorchester Avenue on the east to Boston Street on the west. It was a typical three-decker neighborhood not far from Andrew Square in South Boston. Unfortunately, its wooden structures also offered a spreading fire plenty of space to grow.

When Liam and his team arrived shortly after the alarm went off, being only located a few miles from the scene, they quickly discovered that a fire on the rear porch at 26 Bellflower Street was the genesis of the blaze and it was rapidly spreading to adjoining houses, which literally turned the entire street and the neighborhood into a cauldron of devastation.

Liam looked in awe as the back of a three-decker went up in a sheet of flame in about a minute. There had been a lot of dry weather and there was a steady breeze that day, plus water pressure in the hydrants was low. Liam knew right away he needed help... a lot of help. He made the call and fire engines came from all over Boston.

Surveying what was happening as three-deckers continued to be engulfed in flames, he suddenly heard a shout from the building behind him, a frantic voice saying several firefighters were trapped inside. Not hesitating for a moment, Liam grabbed an axe and ran up the front steps, only to be thrown back momentarily by a blast of hot air. He took a deep breath and plowed through the inferno where he discovered several firefighters had been trapped behind a partially collapsed wall. Swinging his axe as the air continued to become more and more super-heated, he hit the wall several times until there was a space big enough for the two trapped men to exit. They ran for the door with Liam behind them, but before he could make it out, the second floor collapsed above him and Liam felt like the weight of the world had suddenly rained down on him.

Later that night, Liam had a nightmare about bodies being lined up under sheets on a sidewalk. Slowly he walked over to one and pulled it back to reveal a beautiful red-haired girl. As Liam stared down at her—she looked as if she were sleeping—

the girl suddenly opened her eyes and screamed at a startled Liam, *"THIS IS ALL YOUR FAULT!"*

Liam bolted up in his hospital bed, his sheet soaked with perspiration, his breath hot and heavy. A soft hand guided him slowly back down to the pillow. Once back down, Liam looked over to see the smiling face of Father Henry Doherty, the priest at Gate of Heaven Parish in South Boston.

"Whoa, take it easy, laddie... it's just a bad dream."

Liam put his hand to his sweaty brow. "The fire?"

"It was a bad one," Father Doherty said sadly. "There were 27 homes destroyed, 300 people now homeless, maybe 35 or more responders hospitalized."

"No casualties?"

"None... thanks partly to you and the good graces of the Lord. Those two men you saved got out safely." Father Doherty hesitated a moment. "But..."

Liam looked over at him. "But what..." The priest looked down at Liam's lower left leg... or at least where it used to be. Liam followed his gaze, and then his eyes went wide. "Oh, God!"

"They couldn't save the leg below the knee," Father Doherty said softly. "I'm sorry, my boy." But Liam Mulvaney couldn't hear what the priest was saying as the words were drowned out by his own sobbing.

* * * * *

The siren blast from an ambulance racing behind him heading for nearby Massachusetts General Hospital brought Liam back to the moment and the task at hand. Taking a deep breath, he started walking slowly and carefully towards the ruined building, never really sure what he would find inside.

Chapter Three

Fire Investigator
*The primary purposes of a fire investigation is to establish the origin of the fire, determine the likely cause, and thus conclude whether the incident was **accidental, natural or deliberate**. It is vital to establish the cause to ensure similar events do not occur (in the case of natural or accidental) or to allow a legal investigation to be conducted (in the case of deliberate fires).*

Still not sure of the steadiness of the back of the hotel, Liam opted instead to start at the front entrance. When he walked around the corner onto Commonwealth Avenue, he saw the usual assortment of gawkers standing on the grass island that separated the east and westbound traffic. He made a mental note to ask Deputy Chief O'Hara if they took any video of the crowd watching the fire as it unfolded. Very often if there is arson involved the perpetrator would hang around to view his (or her) handiwork. There was also a camera crew from Channel 5 at the scene. Liam recognized the reporter talking into the camera, Natalie Jacobson, who just started at the station a few months ago. A real looker, he thought to himself.

At the bottom of the steps he nodded to a bored-looking uniformed cop who lifted the yellow caution tape to allow Liam access to what was once a grande dame among Boston hotels. But no more. Her day had come and gone. Liam entered her charred remains.

As a fire investigator Liam wore the uniform of his profession; a hardhat, fire-resistant clothing, steel-toed shoes, thick gloves and goggles. Safety was always the key as dangers such as structural collapse, escaping gasses, damaged electricity, debris, asbestos and combustible materials lurked in every corner. Fortunately, Liam knew the gas and electricity had long been turned off; but he was still on guard. Even when a stove is turned off it can still burn you after the fact.

Liam treated every fire investigation like a crime scene, although the statistics were overwhelmingly in favor of the fire's origin being something as innocent as electrical or accidental. At this point the prevailing theory was that a worker had accidentally started the blaze with an errant blow-torch. It was very possible, but Liam couldn't afford to take any shortcuts. He approached every site with the idea there are some very bad people in the world, and then he hoped to prove himself wrong. Because when arson *does* happen, it's usually for the same reasons; insurance fraud or to conceal or cover up a crime. Still, before you can establish whether arson has taken place, you have to first find out the origin of the fire. Right off the bat the region where the fire started usually burns for a longer amount of time, so that's where you will likely find the most damage. The problem is that most of the damage could have been caused by dozens of firefighters wielding axes, rakes and high-pressure water hoses. Nonetheless, the way fire affects certain materials can also be helpful. As a rule, fire burns upwards and outwards, so you will often find V-shaped patterns on surfaces around the origin of the fire. Also, glass and plastic tends to melt in the direction of the fire. Burned wallpaper and drapes can also indicate distinct ignition points.

Liam carefully and methodically walked around the foyer of the hotel, trying hard not to inhale too much of the smell, which reeked of sulfur and burned wood. Thankfully, the smell of burned flesh was not present. That was a smell that entered deep into his nasal passages some 30 years ago and has hung on ever since like a hard-to-reach booger. As is the norm, he first walked the area that showed the least damage, which would help him backtrack to what would be the seat of the fire; that area with the most damage.

With the specter of arson always at the forefront of his thinking, Liam knew from experience that flammable liquids, such as kerosene, gasoline, even turpentine were the arson's "weapon of choice," though it was not common for them to leave behind such damning evidence as an empty gas can. That would be too easy. Yet accelerants can also leave a unique footprint by way of extremely localized burn patterns, such as obvious spaces between the burned and unburned areas and the detection of hydrocarbon vapors, although a sniffer dog would be needed for that and Liam didn't have one handy at the moment.

Liam then advanced to the dining room area where his attention immediately went to a pile of partially charred newspapers in a corner of the room. He found that interesting and made a mental note of it. The investigation went on for the better part of an hour as Liam made meticulous notes but didn't come to any immediate conclusion as to whether or not the fire was deliberately set. Getting ready to leave, his attention was once again drawn to the partially-charred pile of newspapers. Walking over carefully, he looked around the area, noting a good amount of soot and ash had accumulated in the region. Going down to one knee he removed one of his gloves and picked up some of the ash and rubbed it between his fingers. When he let the ash drop from his hands he could feel residue on his fingers. He placed his fingers under his nose and the smell was easily identifiable; petroleum. This fire was definitely not caused by a clumsy worker with a hot blowtorch.

Having taken a sample of the ash as evidence, Liam nodded once again to the cop and exited the building. He took a right at Dartmouth Street and headed back to the rear of the building where he had parked his car. As he approached his 1968 Chevy Malibu he groaned inwardly at the sight of a piece of paper tucked under his windshield wiper, confused as to why the City of Boston would be ticketing on a Sunday morning. Once he reached his car he took the paper from under the wiper and even before he opened the folded piece he knew it wasn't a traffic citation. Unfolding the sheet he read the message scrawled in black letters.

At first Liam was relieved it wasn't a parking ticket and at the same time amused that in all likelihood it was placed there by some hippie, whereas over the past few years there have been more and more anti-war protests popping up in Boston; you couldn't walk down the street without a flower child passing you a flyer. Liam started to crumple the paper, but something far back in the recesses of his brain told him maybe he should hold on to it. He looked at the message once more, folded it and stuffed it in his shirt pocket. The message read:

Ain't it a gas, gas, gas!

Chapter Four

Brighton, MA ... Tuesday, June 20, 1972

Several days after the fire, Liam was sitting in his cubicle at the Massachusetts State Police barracks in Brighton, chewing on a bagel with veggie cream cheese and looking through that morning's *Boston Globe*. Having already perused the sports section and being totally disgusted by the Red Sox loss to the White Sox the day before yesterday by an 8-4 drubbing, although Sox catcher Carlton Fisk *did* hit a monster home run, Liam was now turning his attention to the movie section.

As someone who always enjoyed a good movie, Liam was pleased to see that next weekend the Park Square Cinema was showing a double-feature of *Catch-22* and *M*A*S*H*. As images of Sally Kellerman as Major "Hot Lips" Houlihan danced in his head, a shout from the Captain's office killed the moment and Liam put down his half-eaten bagel and prepared to head for the corner office. As he folded the paper and placed it on his desk his attention focused on a story at the bottom of the front page. The headline read:

"What *REALLY* Happened at the Cocoanut Grove That Fateful Night 30 Years Ago?"

by Robbie Bernstein, Boston Globe Spotlight Team

Liam felt a cold finger trace his spine as he swallowed hard and went to see the Captain.

When Liam entered the office, Captain Jo-Jo Calvino, 300-lbs of muscle and don't-screw-with-me attitude, was seated behind his desk, his sausage-like fingers formed a steeple and his eyes were closed as he appeared to be deep in thought. His eyeglasses sat high up on his bald head. Liam knew from past experience that when the Captain was like this it was best to let him start the conversation. While he stood there patiently, Liam noticed for the first time that he and the Captain were not the only people in the office. He glanced over to see a young Negro man with a medium-sized afro leaning against the wall with his arms folded across his chest. He wore a windbreaker over a tee-shirt and dark jeans. He looked back at Liam but said nothing.

"So, Mulvaney...," the Captain's booming voice brought Liam back to the matter at hand. "Where are we with the hotel fire?"

Liam looked at the other man again. "We sent the evidence to the lab, and as expected the testing came back positive for an accelerant."

"So it was intentionally lit."

"Yes, I believe so."

Calvino nodded his head. "So we have a murder—nine murders."

"Yes," Liam agreed. "Though I would argue they were unintentional."

"How so?"

"Well, the building was for all purposes empty," Liam said. "So I don't think he intended there to be victims."

Calvino wasn't convinced. "We have nine dead firemen, Mulvaney."

"I know, I know… but the perp couldn't have known a wall was going to collapse."

Calvino waved his hand in the air as if shooing away a pesky housefly. "Oh, so you think this was all… *accidental*, do ya?"

"No sir… I think it was practice."

For the first time the other man in the room spoke. "So you think it's a firebug?"

"Yes, I think…" Liam looked hard at the man. "I'm sorry, and you are…?"

"Oh, forgive my social faux pas," Calvino said sarcastically. "Mulvaney, this is Terry Tillman. Tillman recently passed the Fire Investigator exam and moved up here from somewhere in Louisiana."

"Mississippi."

"I don't give a fuck. Seems Tillman here used to be a firefighter down in klansville and the crackers down there weren't too happy to have someone of his colorful persuasion on the local fire department—unless of course their house was on fire." Calvino looked over at Terry. "Do I have that right, Tillman?"

Tillman shrugged. "Close enough... sir."

Calvino leaned back in his chair and spread his arms wide. "But Boston, being a bastion of liberalism and a true fighter for the underdog, has taken young Tillman here to its we-shall-overcome bosom and embraced him. Therefore, he is now a part of the team."

Liam nodded at Tillman. "Welcome aboard."

"And your partner."

Liam whipped his head back in Calvino's direction.

"What? *My partner?*"

"Yes indeed," Calvino said with a big smile spreading across his face. "Wait, I think we're having a kumbaya moment. Can you both feel it? Why, I even envision a new TV sitcom; 'The Mick & the Hick', airing weeknights at 9pm, right after *Mod Squad.*"

"C'mon, Cap... you know I like to work alone," Liam pleaded.

Calvino dropped his smile. "Mulvaney, try to imagine how much I *don't care* what you want; then multiply it by 10."

"But..."

"Now both of you get out of my office and go do your job," Calvino roared, standing up. "Catch that bug before he figures out he's pretty damn good at this thing and burns my city down."

Chapter Five

Chinatown, Boston ... Saturday, June 21, 1972

2:05 a.m.

Unlike San Francisco and New York City, Boston's Chinatown is extremely small, comprised of only a handful of narrow one-way streets that are constantly clogged with traffic. The sidewalks are no better as pedestrians vie for a seat in the numerous restaurants that makes up its lifeblood. You can't walk more than 10 feet in either direction before you're staring into a window and marveling at cooked duck and chicken hanging from hooks, as well as several other unidentifiable unfortunate creatures.

When it comes to eateries, the two big boys on the block are the China Pearl, and directly across the street you'll find the more popular Bob Lee's Islander, with its faux Polynesian decor. The three-story Fung Wong Restaurant, located a few doors down from the China Pearl and next to a gift shop, is hardly in that class, but it still does its share of business between the locals and the tourists. Maybe it's the sign outside that touts "Real Chinese Food," as if the other restaurants somehow sold fake Chinese food.

Along with being a pretty decent restaurant, Fung Wong was also where 17-year-old Zhang Jun worked. But Zhang wasn't a waitress, or even a dishwasher. Zhang Jun worked on the second floor of the restaurant, along with her 14-year-old sister Mai, her mother, Xu, and a dozen other women who all recently journeyed to America from their homes in the Gansu Province of China. All of the women were now sitting at sewing machines in a cramped 20 x 15-foot room located directly above the restaurant's kitchen. There was one metal door that led out to a hallway that housed a small bathroom. The windows could open halfway, and fortunately the metal grating didn't block too much of the infrequent cooling breeze that at least lowered the temperature a few degrees in the stifling hot room. This was the reason the women were working in the early morning hours, as the restaurant had no air-conditioning on the upper floors and the temperature rose dramatically during the summer days.

The restaurant had closed for the evening just after 1 a.m., so the downstairs was deserted. Out the window Zhang could hear late-night passersby and the occasional police siren as she toiled sewing patches on work-clothes. But even through the whirring of a dozen sewing machines, Zhang thought she heard a bang on the metal door (perhaps a late-night employee?). She didn't think too much of it and went back to the job at hand. But after another bang, Zhang looked over at the door, now with an air of concern. Her sister saw her staring and stopped her machine.

"What is it, Zhang?"

She looked at her baby sister and smiled. "Nothing, Mai; go back to work." Her sister did.

A few moments later, Zhang thought she smelled smoke, and wondered if maybe someone had lit a fire in a trash can on the sidewalk below the window. Perhaps an errant cigarette had been tossed by one of the many inebriated college kids still prowling the streets even in the early morning hours. But that thought quickly vanished as smoke started to come up between the cracks in the floorboard. Several women jumped up with a concerned look on their faces, which quickly became cries of panic as the very floor itself seem to transform into a river of fire. Crying out frantically, workers pushed and shoved to get to the lone door, only to find it had been locked from the outside. They banged frantically on it, but to no avail. Some scrambled to the window, using all their strength to pry the metal screen off, but the end result was no more than bloodied fingers. As several crying women held each other and succumbed to the smoke and flames, Zhang, Mai and their mother hugged each other as the flames and thick smoke swallowed them. Zhang's last thought was they should never have left China.

10:15 a.m.

Liam had to admit—albeit somewhat reluctantly—that Tillman wasn't the pain in the ass he expected him to be. They had been partnered up for a few days now and Liam actually found himself *almost* liking him. And he also had to admit it was kind of sweet when his wife, Nina, who was a foot shorter than Tillman but blessed with a pleasant smile, brought him his lunch one day. Sweet… in a dorky sort of way.

That afternoon stuck in Liam's mind for other reasons. Lunch wasn't the only thing Nina Tillman brought to the office that day. She also had with her Tillman's 8-year old daughter, Bessie, clutching tightly to her little chest a Mrs. Beasley doll from some TV show Liam couldn't recall. That day, like clockwork every noontime, Liam would pull up the pants on his left leg and rub salve where the false leg and real leg met. And in his mind today was just a normal day, until he looked over and saw Bessie staring at him wide-eyed. When he looked up and saw her, he quickly pulled the pant leg down.

"Oh, damn!" He looked over at Tillman and Nina. "I'm sorry... I forgot..." But Nina's smile disarmed his awkwardness.

"That's OK, Mr. Mulvaney," she said. "She doesn't need to be sheltered from life."

Bessie walked slowly over to Liam's desk. She looked at him, and then put her little hand on his prosthetic.

"Were you in a war?"

Liam thought carefully how to answer. "In a way."

"Mommy said you were a fireman."

"I was."

"Is that how you hurt your leg?"

Liam felt himself start to choke up a little. "Yes."

She felt the leg again through Liam's pants.

"Will my daddy have a leg like this someday?"

"Bessie!" Tillman's wife said, but a hand on her arm stopped her from continuing.

Liam looked Bessie in the eye. "No, we don't go into fires anymore, me and your daddy. We get there after the fire is out. We just kind of... (he looked over at Tillman who was smiling)... clean up after."

Bessie nodded, the answer seemed to satisfy her. She hugged a startled Liam and went back to her mother.

"Mommy, can we go get ice cream now?"

"What the hell are you listening to?"

Tillman's question brought him back to the present as they headed in Liam's car down Storrow Drive towards Chinatown. The Carpenters were playing on his 8-track player—"Rainy Days and Mondays."

"Damn, man! Let me see what else you got back there," Tillman said as he twisted around and grabbed a handful of 8-tracks off the back seat.

"John Denver... The Bee Gees... *TOM JONES*! Hell, you just might be the whitest person I know!"

"The music soothes me."

"Yeah, right... where are the brothers and sisters?"

"I'm an only child."

"Very funny." Tillman sat back in his seat. "Got any Otis Redding?"

"No."

"Aretha?"

"No."

"James Brown?"

"No."

"Gladys Knight & the Pips?"

"What's a Pip?"

"I give up."

"Forget the music and read the report. Give me the short version." Liam knew this was Tillman's first real fire investigation and he wanted him to focus.

Tillman opened the folder. "Fire started early this morning, approximately 2 a.m., believed to be in the restaurant's kitchen area. Flames worked their way up through the floor and also consumed the second level of the building."

Tillman flipped to the second page, but did not continue. Liam knew why. He looked over at him and saw Tillman staring at the page.

"How many casualties?" Liam asked. Tillman didn't respond.

"Tillman! How many dead?"

He looked up from the sheet and turned to Liam. "Huh... what?"

Liam softened his voice.

"How many victims?"

Looking down he read; "There were 11 bodies found... no 12, one as young as 14." Tillman closed the reports and looked out at the Boston traffic. A few moments passed in silence.

"Welcome to my world," Liam finally said as he searched for a parking spot.

Because the streets in Chinatown were so narrow, and the main street was still clogged with first responder vehicles, Liam found a spot on Kneeland Street and he and Tillman—carrying a bag with their protective gear over his shoulder—walked a block up to Beach Street and to the site of the fire. When they took the corner the first thing they saw was the coroner's van parked beside several bodies covered with sheets that had been lined up on the sidewalk. Liam staggered for a moment, only managing to catch his balance by leaning on a wall. Tillman grabbed his arm.

"Whoa! You okay, man?"

"I'm fine," Liam said, shrugging off his partner's arm. "Just skipped breakfast this morning. Let's go."

As Liam got closer—nodding to a few uniforms he knew—he could see that the restaurant had been gutted by the flames. The front window was gone and food that had been hanging in the window was strewn about the sidewalk. A skinny dog quickly grabbed what was probably once a chicken off the pavement and scurried down the street to enjoy his meal. Rats would come next.

Off to the side Liam and Tillman donned their protective gear and entered what used to be the front of the restaurant. Wood was charred in all directions, while metal—most likely tables and chairs—was twisted by the searing heat. Both men had to navigate slowly through puddles of dirty water.

"What's that smell?" Tillman asked, wrinkling his nose.

"You don't want to know," Liam answered, knowing from experience it would linger in the air for hours even after the bodies were removed. "Popular opinion is that the origin of the fire was the kitchen... let's check it out."

As both men carefully made their way into what remained of the restaurant's kitchen, Liam and Tillman shone their flashlights up to a huge empty hole that once served as the kitchen's ceiling and the second level's floor. All the victims were found on the first level after the floor gave way. The coroner would determine perhaps who was alive and who was dead when the floor caved in, as if it really mattered at this point. Tillman turned the beam of his flashlight towards a metal door covered in thick soot now lying propped against what was once a huge oven. "Look at that," he said. Liam looked.

"Report said there was only one door on the second floor," Liam said, now looking back up at the hole. "Must have come down with the bodies."

Then something caught his eye. He walked over to the door and rubbed his hand over a section where the soot seemed the thickest. In doing so it revealed a thick pouch, which Liam knew was made of asbestos. It was bolted to the outside of the metal door. Carefully, Liam opened the pouch and extracted a piece of paper. Liam didn't believe in coincidences.

Could this be The Last Time?

Chapter Six

Boston… Tuesday, June 27, 1972

Liam passed in his findings on the Chinatown fire to his boss, noting the blaze to be of "suspicious origin." What he did *not* submit, however, were the two notes that had been left behind; the one left at the recent fire and the one at the hotel fire that claimed the lives of nine firefighters on June 17. Both notes were now sitting on the table between Liam and Tillman as they ate lunch at Buzzy's Roast Beef, a favorite place for doctors and nurses at nearby Mass. General to grab a quick lunch. The restaurant was located on Cambridge Street under the Charles Street train station and next to the Charles Street Jail. Atmosphere was not its calling card. But the food was great. Next to Kelly's on Revere Beach; the best roast beef in town.

"Damn, man, are you sure about this?" Tillman asked, pausing from taking another bite of his sandwich, the blood-red meat bursting out of an onion roll and barbeque sauce spilling out of the sides. "I mean, like, this is evidence. Dig?"

Liam rested an elbow on the table and ran his hand through his hair. "I know, I know. But this is something else. It feels... personal."

"Personal?" Tillman said, wiping his mouth with a paper napkin.

"I mean, I think these notes were personally left for me; someone wanted me to have them."

"Why?"

Liam sighed heavily and picked up a french fry. He shook his head. "I don't know." He dipped the fry into a small white paper cup of ketchup and put it in his mouth.

Tillman was still unconvinced. "I kind of dig what you're saying, Liam, but I dunno... withholding evidence. They find out they can shit-can my ass back to Mississippi."

Liam suddenly felt guilty about putting his partner in jeopardy. Still, he felt strongly that the notes were the key to finding this fire-bug and he couldn't relinquish control of them. He had no choice.

"Please, Tillman, work with me on this," Liam pleaded. "At least for a little while longer."

Tillman took a sip of his drink. He placed it back on the table and stared at it. Liam waited.

"Okay," Tillman finally said, still staring at the drink in front of him. "A while longer."

"Thanks."

Tillman then looked at the notes on the table. "What do you think they mean?"

Liam shook his head. "No clue. Riddles were never my thing."

Both men stared at the notes a few minutes more before Tillman said, "Okay, and change of subject. Nina's boss gave her tickets to the Red Sox game on Saturday, and you're going with us."

Liam hesitated. He tried lying. "I hate baseball, and besides I have things to do around my apartment." But Tillman only laughed.

"First of all, I know you like baseball because every morning you have your face buried in the sports section of *The Boston Globe*. Second, I've seen your apartment; it's a dump."

Liam found it hard to argue with either assumption, so he just frowned.

"Sox playing Milwaukee on Saturday; 1 p.m., be there or square," Tillman said. "Luis Tiant pitching—El Tiante—gonna be a great game." He took another bite of his sandwich as Liam gathered up the two notes and put them back in his pocket.

"Besides," Tillman added with a sly smile on his face. "You know how Bessie likes to hang out with her Uncle Liam."

"Shut up and eat your sandwich."

Saturday turned out to be a clear and sunny day with surprisingly low humidity for the first day of July in Boston. Liam, Tillman, Nina and Bessie were seated in the right field grandstand section. As Tillman had predicted, Tiant was pitching a gem and mowing down batters. It was just the fourth inning and already he had eight strikeouts recorded.

Liam looked out at the left field stands, near the Green Monster. Someone had decided to place a big card with the letter "K" on it every time Tiant struck out a batter.

"Liam, I'm going for beer; do you want another Coke?"

"I want cotton candy!" yelled Bessie, looking adorable with her Red Sox cap and waving a huge foam finger.

"I'll get it," Liam said as he stood up, taking one last look over at the K cards across the field. But when he did he staggered and fell back in his seat.

Liam closed his eyes as tight as he could. He felt Bessie's hand on his arm. "Are you okay, Mr. Mulvaney?"

Slowly, he opened his eyes and looked again across the field.

He let out a deep breath and looked down at Bessie, seeing the concerned look on her face. He smiled at her.

"I'm fine," Liam said. "Just lost my balance; darn leg." But as he rose once again he could see people looking out over the center field bleachers, including Tillman. Liam slowly followed their gaze and what he saw was thick black smoke rising in the distance. He sat back down as his stomach tightened. The ballgame no longer seemed to matter.

11:10 a.m.

Two hours before Luis Tiant's first pitch

It wasn't exactly like going to Disneyland, but for three young girls who had just last month graduated from St. Agatha's School in Dorchester, it was a big thrill. When you're looking to grab some quick, cheap clothes for college, there was no better place to be than Filene's Basement, which they nicknamed "Fi Bay."

Ginny Delvecchio, Maura Turner and Karen Carberry had met up at Ashmont Station in the morning and taken the train to the Summer Street stop at the corner of Summer and Washington Streets. Without even going outside they were able to take the old narrow stairs down to the basement, where they were immediately met by the tumult and the shouting of the women's clothing section. For as far as they could see there were tables and bins filled with clothes being picked over by a raucous crowd of shoppers, diving into everything from sweaters and blouses, to scarves and everything else under the sun, plus racks and racks of dresses and more dresses. There were no changing rooms in Filene's Basement so women and girls were trying on things right in the aisles, sometimes stripping first to their underwear while ducking around some column or bin, or not even bothering to do that in the rush. Off to the right a rather large woman was involved in a vicious tug-of-war with a small Asian woman who was not about to give up a pair of plaid slacks. It would be a fight to the death.

"This is so-o-o-o groovy!" Ginny exclaimed as she ventured forth into the mayhem. Karen was a little less enthusiastic. She had claustrophobia and for years had shied away from small

spaces and tight quarters. And with the large crowd of people and low, perhaps only nine-foot ceilings she was trying to hold back a panic attack. Taking a deep breath she looked behind her and saw that Maura was already gleefully going through a table full of sweaters.

After about a half-hour, Ginny had a handful of clothes with her, and Maura found a paisley dress that was "so fab!" As they looked around for where to jump in line for a cash register, Karen suddenly felt a pain in the pit of her stomach as someone yelled out, "There's smoke coming from behind a table in the corner!" The cry was followed by screams as the smoke was now a red-and-orange flame that started to climb the wall and quickly ignited the drop ceiling panels. There were more screams as people started to rush towards one of the exits, but because there were so many people trying to escape the doors quickly became blocked. Bodies piled on bodies.

Maura grabbed Karen's hand and shouted, "C'mon... let's go!" However, Karen was in full panic mode and frozen to her spot. But before Maura could shake her friend from her panicked state, several hysterical women plowed into them and both Maura and Karen hit the floor hard; Ginny was nowhere to be found. Lying on her back, Karen screamed as several more bodies fell on her, their weight pressing down on her slim body. She tried to scream but her chest couldn't expand enough to let out the sound.

Then the lights went out.

Several hours later the fire would get so intense that the thick black smoke could be seen from Fenway Park.

Chapter Seven

Boston... Tuesday, June 27, 1972

The smoke was like a beacon calling Tillman and Liam to its origin. They decided to leave in the fifth inning after giving Nina cab money, telling her that she and Bessie might as well enjoy the rest of the game as chances are it could be a long night. She reluctantly agreed.

Traffic wasn't too bad and Liam made it across town in record time, grabbing a parking spot on Tremont Street not far from Park Street station. They walked several blocks to the downtown area and could see numerous fire apparatus lining the streets as uniformed cops tried to keep the crowd at bay. Liam noticed Deputy Chief O'Hara standing off to the side and approached him. Liam introduced to Tillman. The two men shook hands.

"How you end up working with this guy?" O'Hara asked, nodding at Liam. Tillman smiled.

"Affirmative action."

Liam ignored them. "What do we know so far, Chief?"

"Fire started in Filene's Basement, moved fast, and rapidly sucked up most of the oxygen in such a small space."

"Did it spread beyond the basement?" Tillman asked.

"Fortunately, no, but we did shut down the trains because the tunnels were flooded from the hoses."

Liam then asked the question he dreaded.

"Casualties?"

O'Hara took a notebook from his shirt pocket and flipped open a page. "14 dead; eight from burns and smoke inhalation, six suffocated under bodies. It didn't take long for the bodies to jam the doors what with everyone trying to get out at once."

Liam swallowed as he remembered the Cocoanut Grove fire and seeing dead bodies stacked in the revolving door.

"We have our stuff in my car," Liam said. "Think it's alright to walk the site?"

"I'd give it a few more hours to cool down,' O'Hara answered. "Grab some dinner and come back maybe around 7 p.m.; I'll let who's ever on duty then know you'll be on the job."

Liam looked again at the entrance to Filene's Basement, now covered in soot with its metal doors twisted and hanging off the hinges. As with the other fires he had a very bad feeling.

After downing a burger and a Coke at Bailey's on West Street, and grabbing their gear from the trunk of Liam's car, both men carefully walked the perimeters of the fire. They then descended down the stairs and into the basement. The power had been restored (no one knew why it had initially gone out), and they could see pretty well. They took samples and left around 9:30 p.m.. Liam was feeling better after not finding any notes left behind.

On Monday afternoon Liam went into the office hoping to find on his desk the report of what they had dropped off at the lab late Saturday night. He was feeling encouraged when he approached his desk and saw a manila envelope. But his heart sank when he saw it was addressed to him. There was a smiling face sticker where the address was. He opened the envelope carefully after donning gloves and dumped out a piece of paper. It fell on his desk and Liam could plainly read:

I think what's puzzling you is the nature of my game.

Liam looked around the office quickly. It was early and only a few people were in. He saw Jerry Sinclair reading *The Boston Herald Traveler* and yelled over.

"Hey, Jer... did you see who dropped this envelope on my desk?" Jerry looked up.

"No, man," Jerry said, still reading his paper. He turned the page. "I think it was already there when I got in about an hour ago."

Liam sat down at his desk, staring at the letter. He felt his hand start to tremble, a feeling he hadn't experienced since his drinking days. Beads of perspiration pop on his brow and wiped them with the back of his sleeve. Liam felt like the world was shrinking in on him, making it hard to catch his breath. Putting the letter in the top drawer of his desk, he then hurried out of the office, passing a startled Jerry Sinclair, and made it quickly to the parking area where he jumped into his car. He knew what his destination was.

Less than an hour later Liam sat in his favorite booth at the L Street Tavern in South Boston. This place had been his favorite hideaway for many years, always savoring in the smells of bleach and beer, throwing back 25-cent drafts with wild abandon, peanut shells crunching under his feet. There was definitely a familiarity about the bar, including the beer that sat in front of him, just as it had in a darker past. At the moment it was untouched.

It had been nearly five years since he last sat in this very same booth, as being now sober all that time meant there was no need to frequent this particular establishment. So what drove him today to re-enter that sad phase of his life, order a beer and take it over to this particular booth? The answer was an easy one; people were dying and he couldn't find a way to stop it.

Perhaps it was his imagination, maybe his brain playing tricks, but the bottle seemed closer to him, beckoning him, inviting him *("What's the harm; just a sip.")*. Liam could feel his *resolve* start  to *dissolve*. He could smell the hops, the barley... *the alcohol!* His right hand that had once been in his lap was now on the table, dangerously close to that final temptation. Less than a foot to that liquid paradise.

Liam looked down at his right hand, at first confused as to why it was clenched. But when he slowly opened it he saw why.

There in his palm was his lucky penny, but it wasn't just an ordinary penny, it was in fact a one pence coin encased in green marble that had been mined in Connemara, a region just northwest of Galway, Ireland. Liam smiled and gave the penny a twirl on the table, thinking back to the last time he sat in this booth.

* * * * * *

"RED SOX WIN, BABY!"

The shout from the bar at the L Street Tavern made Liam bolt up in his booth, where he had nearly passed out. On the table in front of him was a dozen empty glasses that had once been filled with draft beer. Most people know where they were when JFK was assassinated. But every die-heart Red Sox fan would remember today, Sunday, October 1, 1967, as the day Jim Lonborg pitched a beauty of a game and made certain the Red Sox were headed for their first World Series since 1946. A 21-year drought.

Liam methodically took each glass and poured whatever was left into one glass, which gave him another half-filled glass of his favorite beverage. His left leg started to ache, but he knew that wasn't possible as a prosthetic limb continued the journey from his left knee to the floor. Phantom pain they called it. As he downed the glass of beer he thought back to the month he spent in the hospital following his accident in 1964, and the year of pain that stretched his body to the limit while rehabilitating. But even more he thought of the misery and guilt and the many, many drinks that consumed his life for nearly two years after he lost his leg, while choosing not to look for work and live minimally on his workers' compensation checks.

Liam had also chosen not to try to venture into any real relationships, feeling undeserving of any real love as he knew it would only end in more misery. Liam Mulvaney was totally convinced that his face was on fate's dart board and every time it hit a bulls-eye a little more of his humanity would be ripped from his body. And so, to appease any carnal urges, he chose to partake in an endless stream of prostitutes. It was all he deserved. And just to jump even more on the misery pig-pile, his mother had suffered a stroke in 1966 and was currently residing at the Marian Manor Nursing Home, the only place that would take her on welfare. Maybe Liam didn't deserve better, but she certainly did. BULLS-EYE! Good shot, fate.

Standing on unsteady feet, Liam took a moment to compose himself. He then worked his way through the raucous crowd four deep at the bar and made his exit into the early-October afternoon. It was 5 p.m. and already dusk was settling in. The air had a chill so he pulled up his collar and made his way the five blocks up to Gate of Heaven Church on Fourth Street, where he knew the 4 p.m. mass had already ended and the church would be empty. He hoped so because he knew what he had to do.

Fifteen minutes later (and after one quick stop to wretch into a trash can where someone had spray-painted "Make Love, Not War" on it) Liam stood in front of the church and looked up at the magnificent stained glass windows. It gave him a moment of comfort, but then it quickly faded. He took the stairs (he was managing his false leg better than he anticipated; one saving grace) and opened the huge wooden doors and entered. As he had anticipated, the church was empty. Liam ventured down to a pew in front (his false limb preventing him from genuflecting) and sat down. Looking up at the giant crucifix hanging over the altar, Christ's face looked at him accusingly. He closed his eyes tight. He tried to think of anything good that had happened in his life—slim pickings—but all he saw were bodies on a sidewalk. He felt a lone tear drop from his eye.

"Liam Mulvaney... is that you?"

Liam opened his eyes and saw Father Henry Doherty standing next to him. He knew the priest because not only was he the pastor at Gate of Heaven, Father Doherty was also the chaplain assigned to the station house where Liam once worked. He was also the first person he saw when he woke up that night in the hospital after the accident that claimed part of his left leg. Liam attempted a smile.

"Hello Father."

Father Doherty smiled back. "I'd ask where you've been these days, but judging by the smell I am guessing it could be any saloon within 10 blocks of here."

Liam let his head drop. "Yeah, well it's been a tough time."

"Maybe something you want to talk about?"

Liam's shoulders heaved as a sob left his throat.

"I've done something terrible, Father."

"Perhaps it would make you feel better to get it off your chest, in the confessional."

"I don't deserve to feel better."

"Rubbish! No one deserves to live in constant turmoil and pain. Come with me." And with that the priest led Liam over to the confessional, where knowing that he would never violate the sanctity of the confessional, he told Father Doherty everything about what happened the night of the Cocoanut Grove fire, and the role he played.

When he was through, Liam sat in the confessional, the priest silent on the other side of the partition. There was quiet for a few minutes before Father Doherty spoke up.

"Liam, I would never reveal to anyone about what happened 25 years ago as I've taken an oath as a priest not to, but perhaps you should report it to the police about who was actually to blame."

Liam shook his head. "I can't. There are other people at risk besides myself. This is on me!" And with that Liam walked as quickly as he could out of the confessional and left the church. Father Doherty didn't go after him, but he knew he had to make a phone call.

Shaken by what just happened, Liam walked a block up to East Broadway and hailed a taxi. He needed to go where misery deserves company. Once he told the driver his destination, he adjusted his prosthetic leg, put his head back, closed his eyes and tried to ignore the chatter from the front seat about how happy his driver was that the 1967 Red Sox were finally going to the World Series once again.

Fifteen minutes later the taxi pulled up to the corner of Washington and Kneeland Streets and Liam exited a few feet from Boston's notorious Combat Zone.

There was no denying that the Combat Zone had a way of getting into a person's blood, and Liam had come here often to get his transfusion of misery. The streets were populated by people who all looked like the walking dead, as if God had taken a giant vacuum cleaner and sucked out all the hope and humanity from anyone who dare venture down its dirty streets.

Liam walked up Washington Street where the neon lights were already starting to glitter as darkness approached. He walked past the giant Liberty Book Store. The store was a safe haven for perverts; you could get lost wandering the long, overstocked aisles. Filling the shelves were every pornographic movie and magazine ever produced, catering to every sort of fetish. There were sex toys and life-size inflatable love dolls and dildos in all shapes, sizes and colors. One-stop shopping. Liam paused briefly at the window, and then continued up the street. Up ahead he could see several of the area's many movie theatres, like the Publix and the Pilgrim, once grand movie theatres but now catering to the raincoat crowd with marquees touting X-Rated films. Although the extremely popular Silver Slipper and the Intermission Lounge beckoned to him, Liam set his sights on The Naked I strip club, which proudly advertised "Totally NUDE College Girl Review."

Three hours and a half-dozen overpriced drinks later, Liam sat at his table, his brain encased in an alcohol fog, watching an endless parade of bored dancers doff their clothes to the pulsating beat of some obscure psychedelic song that sounded vaguely familiar. The day-long drinking binge started to pickle his brain while conjuring up horrible memories. He shut his eyes as tight as he could, hoping to squeeze the nightmarish images out of his head. But when he opened them all he could see was a skinny girl dancing around a pole, her red hair tossed about her face, barely held in place by a bright green ribbon.

"I can save her," Liam muttered to himself. "I can save her." He staggered to his feet and made his way towards the stage. The girl stopped dancing, her face looking concerned as this drunk tried to climb on the stage. She had seen this before; a hazard of the profession. But she had never seen a guy with such pleading eyes. But before she could react any further, the man was pulled back by a large muscular bouncer wearing a Led Zeppelin tee-shirt that barely concealed his muscles.

73

"Hey, sit down buddy, or you're out of here!"

But Liam felt he was on a mission of redemption as he whirled around and caught the bouncer full in the mouth with his elbow, causing him to stagger back. Turning, Liam continued towards the stage but suddenly felt himself buried under several bodies.

For almost 24 hours Liam sat in a dirty cell at Police Headquarters on Berkeley Street. The judge, taking into consideration Liam was a former firefighter and had been hurt in the line of duty, set his bail low at $200. Since Liam had no money and few if any friends, so he fully expected to spend some additional time behind bars. But that didn't happen.

"Okay, Mulvaney... you're out of here. Bail's been posted," said a policeman as he unlocked the cell.

Shocked because he didn't know of anyone who had $200, let alone anyone would want to waste it on his sorry ass, Liam gathered up his jacket and walked out to the waiting area, where he saw a young man with long hair and a mustache. He wore a green army jacket, jeans and boots. Liam walked over to him.

"Who are you?"

74

The man extended his hand and smiled. Liam hesitated but the man left it out there. Finally, Liam gripped it.

"My name is Caleb McNab," he said. "I'm a friend of Father Doherty."

"You know Father Doherty?"

"I do, he helped me out when I was having some... issues."

"Issues?"

"I was in Vietnam in '65, saw a lot of bad shit, came home with baggage, and thought I'd be better off with a bullet in my head. Talked myself out of it by trying to drink myself to death; just a slower form of suicide, really."

"How did you know I was here?"

Caleb chuckled. "Father called me after you left, told me to follow you. Which I did. Took me a day or so to raise the money for the bail."

"I'll pay you back."

"No, you won't. Anything you have will go to a bottle or a hooker."

"Fuck you."

Caleb smiled. "Hey, the truth hurts. But I tell you what; there is a way you can pay me back?"

"Yeah, what's that?"

Caleb took out a card and handed it to him. "See that address on Boylston Street. The day after tomorrow we have our weekly meeting of AA... be there."

Liam looked at the card with every feeling in his body telling him to rip it up and throw it in this arrogant asshole's face. But he didn't.

"I'll expect to see you," Caleb said as he started for the front door of the station. As he did he took a moment to pause and yell over his shoulder. "The Red Sox in the World Series. Man, who would have thought it? It doesn't get much cooler than that."

Liam did show up that day for his first meeting, and for the rest of 1967 and until the spring of 1968 he attended every session faithfully. Caleb also got him a part-time job working the front desk at the Boston Public Library. And on May 12, 1968, Liam and Caleb celebrated Liam's successful completion of AA's

12-step program with a steak at Jacob Worth's Restaurant in the Theatre District, where Caleb raised a toast to his friend.

"To Liam Mulvaney and new beginnings."

Liam raised his iced tea and clinked glasses. "Thanks, Caleb."

"And now, my sober friend," said Caleb. "I have a surprise." He took an envelope out of his pocket and slid it across the table.

Liam looked at it. "What's that?"

Caleb shrugged and bit into his steak. "Think of it as a graduation present."

Liam opened the envelope and took out a letter. He read it carefully, and then looked at Caleb who was smiling slyly.

"How did you manage this?"

"I know you loved being a firefighter, and I figured this was the next best thing considering your... ahem, limitations."

"I can't believe this."

"You have four months to study for the exam. And I have no doubt you'll make an excellent fire investigator."

Liam felt himself choking up. "I... I..." Caleb held up his hand, the look on his face taking a serious tone.

"There's one thing you have to always remember, Liam... you're an alcoholic. Every day you will be tested. Demons will lurk in the shadows, trying to pull you into their darkness. They want your soul."

"I know."

"So anytime you feel like you're slipping, look at this and let it be a reminder of where you once were." And with that Caleb placed a round object on the table. To Liam it looked like a penny encased in green marble. Caleb pointed at it.

"That's a one pence coin surrounded by marble mined from Connemara, where my people are from in Ireland. Keep it with you always."

Liam picked up the coin and grasped it in his fist.

"Thank you, Caleb, for everything."

"You're welcome, boyo," Caleb said. "Now finish your dinner and go home; you have a lot of studying to do."

* * * * *

Now sitting in his booth looking down at the lucky charm Caleb gave him four years ago, Liam smiled. But there was also a degree of sadness; his friend passed away in 1970 from bladder cancer caused by the effects of Agent Orange used in Vietnam. He missed him deeply. But Liam knew what he had to do, and it didn't involve what was sitting in front of him. Smiling, Liam pushed the bottle back across the table. He stood up, looked around the L Street Tavern for one last time, and left to do his job.

Chapter Eight

Boston... Monday, August 7, 1972

Liam Mulvaney sat at his desk reading the newspaper's sports section and wondering if the Red Sox actually had a chance this year. After the Filene's Basement fire the rest of July had been relatively quiet. He and Tillman investigated a half-dozen situations, but all proved either to be accidental or electrical. The one exception was a guy who set his neighbor's house on fire because their dogs barking kept him awake all night.

Still, the city had its fair share of excitement. Along with the perennial demonstrations against the war and President Nixon that took place on the Boston Common (all relatively peaceful, although one idiot dumped boxes of soap detergent in the Frog Pond), for three days Boston's South End section erupted during a Puerto Rican Day celebration. According to a report Liam had read in *The Boston Globe*, a fight grew into a confrontation between bystanders and more than 100 policemen. Mostly young Puerto Ricans set buildings on fire, damaged police cruisers and stoned passing cars. The police were criticized for aggravating the situation. Luis Palmarin, a South End resident, told the *Globe*: "The cop arrested me when I tried to stop him from beating a man who was bleeding badly. He threw me in the car, grabbed a soda bottle from the floor, called me a spic and hit me in the face with the bottle." Of course, Boston City Councilman Albert "Dapper" O'Neil made the situation worse by ordering the police to "club those maggots and leeches out of the park." The stupidity of some people continued to boggle Liam's mind.

The relative calmness made Liam consider that maybe, *just maybe*, the arsonist, and his cryptic notes were finished, and that maybe he moved on to burn down some other city. But deep in his heart Liam knew this was unlikely; and then the phone rang.

"Mulvaney," Liam answered, still looking down at the box-score of yesterday afternoon's game against Detroit.

"Just the man I was trying to reach," responded a pleasant voice on the other end of the phone.

"Well, you reached him," Liam said, still scanning the pages of the newspaper. "Who's this?"

"My name is Robbie Bernstein, and I'm with *The Boston Globe.*"

Liam looked up from his newspaper. Why did the name sound familiar? His radar was activated but Liam tried not to sound nonplussed.

"What a coincidence; I was just reading your paper."

"We appreciate your loyalty," Robbie said. "I'm working on a story for the *Globe*'s Spotlight Team." Liam recalled the story in the paper, an investigation into the Cocoanut Grove deaths, but decided to play dumb.

"And what would that be?"

"Well, I'm sure you're familiar with the Cocoanut Grove nightclub fire 30 years ago, where a lot of people died." Liam felt his stomach clench.

"I am," he replied. "What's it got to do with me?"

"It seems that when I went through some of the employee records that were recovered at the scene—those that were locked in a metal safe—I saw the name Liam Mulvaney pop up. Didn't think much of it until I saw your name in the paper last month as the lead investigator on both the Chinatown fire and the Filene's Basement tragedy." There was a pause, but Liam chose not to respond. "You are one and the same; am I correct?" Robbie inquired.

Liam sighed and knew it wasn't worth the effort to deny the fact. "I am."

"Great," Robbie said enthusiastically. "I would love to pick your brain about that night."

"Why so interested in something that happened 30 years ago?" Liam countered. "Didn't they say it was an accident?"

"So they say," Robbie said. "But I have my doubts. So what do you say, how about I buy you lunch today?"

Liam hesitated. "I don't know... it's pretty busy..." But Robbie Bernstein would not be denied.

"C'mon, everyone eats lunch," Robbie said pleasantly. "How about 2 p.m. at the Aku Aku in Cambridge? Who doesn't like a good pupu platter!"

Liam sighed again, this time even more heavily. He knew this guy wasn't going away.

"Sure, 2 p.m."

"Great! See you then." Robbie hung up.

Liam put the phone back on the cradle and leaned back in his chair. He rubbed his eyes and thought to himself, "Good Lord, what am I getting myself into?"

The Aku Aku was pretty crowded for a Monday afternoon, mostly with businessmen and students all on a frantic quest for good dumplings as if they were searching for the Holy Grail. Liam sat across from Robbie at a table in the corner and watched the *Globe* reporter go to town on a spare rib. Robbie Bernstein wasn't very tall and he had a very slim build. Liam took him to be in his early 40s. He wore a blue pinstripe shirt and a yellow bow-tie with suspenders. His hair was thin and he seemed to be prematurely balding. His glasses sat atop his head.

"So, Liam… can I call you Liam?"

"Sure."

"Tell me what you know about that night."

Liam grabbed a crab rangoon and put it on a small plate in front of him. "Pretty much what everyone else knows; there was a tragic fire and nearly 500 people died."

Robbie wiped his mouth with a napkin. "Did you also know at the same time there was a bank heist downtown?"

Liam still stared at the uneaten appetizer. "No, I didn't."

"Well, there was. A big one." Robbie broke an eggroll in half. "Don't you think that's a mighty big coincidence?"

"I guess."

"Well, Liam, I'm a journalist and I tend not to believe in coincidence." He held up half an eggroll and gestured it towards Liam, who shook his head. "I believe, and what I and my team hope to prove, is that the Cocoanut Grove fire was a distraction, a tragic distraction, and that the fire was deliberately lit."

"You make this sound almost personal."

"Well," Robbie said, looking at Liam. "It is in a way. You see, I was 12 that night, and my big sister, who was 17, worked at the Cocoanut Grove. She died that night."

Liam wasn't sure what to say. "I'm sorry."

"Maybe you knew her, since the records show you worked that night."

"No, I don't think so," Liam said. He smiled a little. "Actually, I didn't think there were any Jews working there."

Now it was Robbie's turn to smile as he grabbed a pork strip from the flaming carousel. "Actually it's kind of an interesting story. After my sister died, my father went out for a pack of smokes and never came back. So me and my mom upped and moved to New York City. While there my mother remarried, her new husband was a man named Morey Bernstein. Morey was a good man and he didn't mind that my mom came with baggage, so to speak, and he raised me like his own. He even paid to send me to journalism school at Columbia University. Sadly, Morey died of a heart attack, and when he did I took his last name as my own, even though I knew it might create 'barriers' going forward." Robbie took a bite of his pork stip. "So from that day on I was no longer Robbie Regan. But I would never forget my red-haired sister, Peggy."

Liam knocked over his water glass. Robbie jumped back in his seat. "Whoa, you okay?"

Liam grabbed a napkin and soaked up the water.

"Sorry...Peggy Regan, red hair, liked to wear a green bow?"

Now it was Robbie's turn to look startled. "You knew her?"

"Not really; just to say hello to." Liam chose not to mention they had a date planned before... He felt himself starting to sweat.

Robbie wiped his hands and took a notebook out of the inside pocket of his sports coat which was hung on the back of his chair. He opened it and started jotting down notes.

"Did you notice anything strange that night, or out of the ordinary?" Robbie was now in full reporter mode. "Anybody suspicious hanging around the nightclub."

"Not that I noticed," Liam answered. This was going badly.

"There was some scuttlebutt that 'Fitzy' Fitzroy might have been involved."

"I've never met the Conor Fitzroy," Liam lied.

Robbie stopped writing and looked up at Liam. "I didn't mention Conor Fitzroy. I said 'Fitzy' Fitzroy."

Liam tried to regain his composure by attempting a smile. "Sorry, I must have misheard you." Robbie continued to stare hard at him. Liam stood up from the table. "Look, thanks for lunch, but I really have to get back to the office."

"Sure," Robbie said. "Thanks for meeting me." He handed Liam his business card. "Maybe you can give me a call if anything comes to mind about that night." Liam took the card, but Robbie held on to the other end. "My sister died that night and someone was responsible... and I *will* find out the truth." He released the card.

"I'm sure you will," Liam said. He took the card and left.

Chapter Nine

On Thanksgiving night in 1942, Boston was all abuzz. On Washington Street, klieg lights traced the star-filled sky and the sidewalk outside the RKO-Keith Theatre was jammed with movie fans and local politicians and celebrities, all full of anticipation as they awaited the Boston premier of the new Humphrey Bogart movie, *Casablanca*.

The film was directed by Michael Curtiz, and starred Humphrey Bogart, Ingrid Bergman, and Paul Henreid. Filmed and set during World War II, it focused on an American expatriate (Bogart) who must choose between his love for a woman (Bergman) and helping her husband (Henreid), a Czechoslovak resistance leader, escape from the Vichy-controlled city of Casablanca to continue his fight against the Germans.

The RKO-Keith was the perfect location for the premier. It was a lavish theatre boasting three-levels of plush seats, a large screen, gold-plated ceilings and side boxes on both sides. Those boxes were reserved for the more important guests, particularly Boston Mayor Maurice J. Tobin and the newly-minted Governor of the Commonwealth of Massachusetts, Leverett Saltonstall, who three weeks earlier barely beat out Roger Pullman in the gubernatorial race.

Of course, a box was also reserved for Danny "Fitzy" Fitzroy, who happened to own a controlling interest in the movie theatre and was overseeing the delivery of the film to the theatre's projectionist. He had tasked his son, Conor, with making sure the film got delivered on time, and after the show making equally sure it was stored for safekeeping at Fitzroy's home in South Boston. As a matter of fact, just to hedge against the film breaking, he had two copies delivered to the projection booth.

Three hours later, the film now over and the Mayor and Governor having finished their posing for photographers from *The Boston Globe* and *The Boston Traveler,* Fitzroy asked Conor if the meeting with the kid from the Cocoanut Grove had been set for Saturday morning. Fitzroy knew it was going to be a very busy and hopefully lucrative weekend and he didn't need any missteps. Conor assured his father that everything was set;

no problems. Liam Mulvaney would be at the meeting, Conor said, "or he would kick his ass."

Saturday, August 19, 1972

Opened in 1920, The Broadway Theatre, located at 420 West Broadway in South Boston, at the corner of F Street and directly across from a Woolworth's, had fallen on hard times. In the 1940s and 1950s it had shown first run films, but since the mid-1960s it was relegated to second-run films (*Ryan's Daughter*), low-budget horror flicks (*Blood of Dracula's Castle*) and violent biker pictures (*Cycle Savages*).

In addition, the interior was in desperate need of some tender loving care. Still, the owner, Manny Zarnoch, loved the old building and was hoping one day to restore it to its natural architectural beauty. This is why he felt a perfect opportunity had fallen in his lap.

About a month ago Manny was approached by a person who told him that, like himself, he loved old movies theatres and he felt he had something that might work for the Broadway Theatre. Turns out this person was in possession of a pristine print, an original mind you, of the classic Bogart movie,

Casablanca (which just happened to be one of Manny's favorite movies), and since 1972 was the 30th anniversary of when it premiered in Boston, what better time to show it again. Manny loved the idea.

As a promotional gimmick, Manny priced the tickets at just $2.00 each, with the hopes of packing the 1,700-plus seat theatre. And Manny got his wish. The turnout was beyond what he imagined; 30 minutes before the 7:30pm start time the place was packed with all types of people; older folks who remembered seeing the movie when it was first released in 1942, and younger people who remember hearing about it from their parents.

And, after all, Bogie was the epitome of cool.

Around 7:10 p.m., in the projection booth above the balcony, 65-year old Ernie Balducci, who had been working the projector at the theatre since 1940, opened the canisters that contained the film. Since hearing that he would be showing an original print of the 1942 film, Ernie had felt very uneasy. As a student of the film processing techniques that had evolved throughout the years, Ernie knew that cellulose acetate was now the material films were being made from.

Ernie looked again at the film canisters and frowned. But whereas his mind was so transfixed on what he was looking at, he didn't detect that someone had quietly entered the booth behind him. And just as Ernie Balducci sensed a presence behind him, a stiletto went deep into the back of his neck. Ernie jolted upright for a moment, and then fell off to the side, blood now flowing from the fatal wound.

The man who ended Ernie's life looked down for a moment at the lifeless body, and then proceeded to take out the spools of film and unravel them so they fell about the floor of the projection booth like strands of shiny brown spaghetti. He took a moment to snip a foot of the film and stick it in his pocket. He then walked to the door, looked back at everything he had accomplished, and then proceeded to take a cigarette lighter out of his pocket. It took two or three spins of the wheel before a blue flame emerged. He then tossed the lit lighter on to the pile of film and hurriedly shut the door behind him as he exited.

Walking quickly down the corridor past the closed doors leading into the auditorium, the man could hear the excited crowd inside waiting with great anticipation for the start of a film that was never going to start. He then bent down and took out several chains that he had strategically hidden behind four-foot high trash canisters and locked as many double doors as he could. He moved quickly because he knew how fast everything was going to happen. Now finished, the man rushed out a side exit and smiled as already he could hear the first screams starting.

Liam and Tillman arrived early the next morning to investigate the scene. They met with Captain Jeffrey DiNicola, who headed up the Boston Police Department's District 6 Station on D Street, a few blocks away. The trio stood off to the side looking at the smoldering building. Liam knew he had to ask the inevitable.

"How many?"

DiNicola let out a breath. "In all, 29, with another dozen being treated at Boston City Hospital."

Liam looked again at the structure and nodded. "Anything else I should know before we head in." Liam and Tillman were already dressed in their protective gear. DiNicola took out a small notebook.

"Reports say Manny Zarnoch—the theater owner—was about to signal up to the projection booth, which is located behind a wall above the back row of the balcony, to begin the movie. At first he thought he saw smoke coming from openings in the wall, where the movie projects from, and then... and I quote... 'An orange light'."

"Orange light?" Tillman said.

"Yup, that's what he said." DiNicola continued to read his notes. "And according to Zarnoch, the back wall pretty much blew out, taking out everyone in the back row and then the flames started traveling across the ceiling. Then... and again I quote... 'All hell broke loose.'" He closed his notebook and put it in his pocket.

"Anything else?" Liam asked.

"Yeah, several doors up in the balcony were chained from the outside."

"Well, I guess we can put a mark in the arson checkbox," Tillman said.

"I guess," Liam answered. "But what caused that back wall to blow out like that?"

"A bomb?" DiNicola offered.

Liam shrugged. "Maybe." He grabbed his bag off the sidewalk. "C'mon, let's go to work." Both men shook DiNicola's hand and started to work their way towards the movie theatre and what was left of the projection booth.

With Liam's leg, it took a little longer than expected to make their way up to the booth, which was pretty much just a hole in a wall now. As they gingerly walked among the debris, they saw a large piece of twisted metal that was partially melted.

"Projector," Liam said, knowing what Tillman was thinking. "Intense heat turns metal into pretzels." They also came across a pile of bones covered in ash and dust.

"The projectionist?" Tillman asked.

"Yup. Ernie Balducci. Pretty much works the same on the human body." Liam went silent and started to look around at what was left of the walls and ceiling. Tillman saw him and asked, "What are you thinking?"

"Flash fire," Liam said. "Oxygen and fuel mix together and come into contact with a heat source that sparks a fire characterized by high heat temperatures and rapid movement."

"So we need to figure out the heat source," Tillman said. He looked around. "A lot of heat, by the looks of this."

"So it would appear," Liam said. "Let's get started."

A few hours later, having finished their initial investigation and feeling no closer to finding answers than when they first started, Tillman and Liam were across the street at the Elite Restaurant having lunch. On a small TV on the wall over a counter, President Richard Nixon was outlining his campaign strategy for the upcoming November election for President. Liam thought to himself he'd heard it all before.

Liam was just about to bite into a burger when a young boy of about 12 approached their table. He was wearing a Red Sox cap and had a pouch slung over his shoulder filled with the *Boston Sunday Globe*. He placed a manila envelope on their table.

"A man told me to give you this," the boy said.

Liam looked at the envelope. He turned to the boy.

"Who gave you this?"

The boy shrugged. "I dunno... some guy, just said give this to you. Gave me two dollars."

"What did he look like?"

"I dunno."

"Big or small," Liam asked, his voice rising.

"I dunno... maybe kinda big." The boy pointed to the area below his ear. "He had some kind of big mark right around here on the left side of his face, all kind of purple and wrinkled. Grossed me out."

"Negro or Caucasian?"

The boy's brow wrinkled in confusion. Tillman jumped in. "Did he look like me, or did he look like him?"

The boy pointed at Liam.

"What color was his hair?" Liam near shouted. "Did he wear glasses? *WHAT DID HE SOUND LIKE?*"

"Liam," Tillman said softly.

Liam whipped his head towards his partner. "WHAT?" Tillman looked at the boy. So did Liam. What he saw made his heart drop; the young boy looked terrified, partly because Liam was shouting at him, and also because he had a tight grip on the boy's arm.

"I'm sorry," he said softly, letting the boy go. The boy quickly left; glad to be away from this madman.

Liam looked at the envelope and took out a pair of gloves from his pocket. He put them on and opened the envelope, taking out a piece of paper. He read it and then handed it to Tillman.

The fire is sweeping our very streets today.

"This guy is a real piece of work, man," Tillman exclaimed.

"There's more," Liam said. Slowly, he pulled out a length of movie film, perhaps 12 inches long.

"Well, that's different," Tillman said. "So, what's it all about, Alfie?"

"Not sure," Liam answered. "But you can bet it has to do with across the street." Liam held the film up to the light.

"Any idea what movie it's from?"

"No," Liam replied. "I can't tell."

"Maybe the clue isn't what movie it's from," Tillman said. "Maybe the clue is the film itself."

"Or maybe both." Liam put the film back in the envelope and removed his gloves. "I know its Sunday, but do you think there's anyone in the lab?"

Tillman thought for a moment. "Maybe Goldman; I don't think he has a life."

Liam nodded. "Okay, let's see what he can tell us."

To save some time, Liam decided to take Beacon Street over to Storrow Drive and out to Brighton. But what they hadn't anticipated, or perhaps merely forgotten, was that there was a huge anti-war rally underway on the Boston Common, and it was spilling on to Beacon Street and snarling traffic. As Liam inched his car by protestors chanting slogans and carrying signs that read *What if they gave a war and nobody came* and *Tricky Dick is the Devil*, it took him nearly an hour to make it to his office.

Fortunately, Nate Goldman was in his lab and was now looking at the film strip that Liam had handed him.

"Fascinating," Goldman said. "I haven't seen this in over 30 years."

Tillman was confused. "What do you mean; it's a piece of film." Nate Goldman removed his thick glasses and smiled at him.

"Oh, this isn't an ordinary piece of film, my Nubian friend," Goldman said. "But perhaps a little history is in order." He sat down in a chair, clearly enjoying the moment. "First off, film today is made from cellulose acetate, and has been since the mid-1950s. Now this print here is made from a base of nitrocellulose, a close relative to gunpowder. Nitrate, as it's commonly known, was the earliest mass-produced celluloid format, and the dominant motion picture medium from 1895 to 1948. Filmmakers and studios loved it for the beauty and clarity of its images. But they soon found out that nitrate is as flammable and physically unstable as my first wife, and to that point it had to be discontinued. Why, the heat from just a cigarette is enough to make nitrate catch fire, and once it does, the flame is extremely powerful."

"How powerful?" Tillman asked.

"So powerful, my friend, that it'll burn underwater."

Tillman's eyes widened. "You're shittin' me!"

"Hypothetically," Liam asked. "What if, say a roomful of this film caught fire?"

"My opinion?" Goldman said. "A mini-Armageddon. By the way, where did you get this film? I thought it was all locked away in a vault somewhere out west."

"It was shown at a theatre in Southie last night," Tillman responded. "I think it was *Casablanca*."

"What a coincidence," Goldman exclaimed. "I was just thinking of that movie. My mother took me and my sister to the Boston premier of Casablanca when I was just 15 years old."

"That was, what, 1941?" Tillman asked.

Goldman shook his head. "No, no… I remember it perfectly. It was Thanksgiving night in 1942. I remember it well because there was a big fire two days later at a nightclub. The… the…" Goldman struggled to remember, snapping his fingers.

"The Cocoanut Grove," Liam said softly.

"That's it!" Goldman proclaimed happily. "Do you remember it?"

Liam didn't respond; he just turned and walked out of the room.

Chapter Ten

It didn't seem possible, Liam told himself as he walked to his car. The last he heard of Conor Fitzroy he was in Ireland. Now all of a sudden, 30 years later, he's back in Boston and lighting fires... *and killing people.* Why? It made no sense. Still, deep in the recesses of Liam's mind he knew that Conor was trouble from the first time he saw him as a kid (Liam's stomach flipped at the memory of that poor dog). Liam also knew that only one person would know if Conor were back and where he was at this very moment. It was not a conversation he wanted to have, at least not if it went at all like the previous one 16 years ago.

* * * * *

March 17, 1956 was a festive day for South Boston as thousands of party-goers had earlier in the afternoon lined the streets of the neighborhood to celebrate St. Patrick's Day. It was just after 7:30 p.m. and the revelers, now fully primed, had spilled into the side streets to keep the celebration going with numerous house parties. It seemed you couldn't walk by a three-decker without hearing the sounds of Ireland blaring from windows.

For Liam Mulvaney it was a night to celebrate for a different reason. At the age of 31 he came in just one year under the maximum age of 32 to be a Boston Firefighter, and yesterday he had passed his exam.

It had been a long, less-than-perfect route to this point in his life. After leaving the Army in 1945, Liam took on a series of rather dangerous jobs. He briefly became an ironworker in the city and walked the steel beams 30 stories above the ground. He worked for a while up in Maine cutting down and hauling trees to lumber yards. And he even did a short stint on a fishing boat up in Gloucester, where he spent some very cold days on very rough waters hauling in lobsters one brutal winter. These weren't jobs that an ordinary person might pursue, but that person didn't carry the mental baggage of Liam Mulvaney. A death wish? He never thought of it that way. Maybe more like a penance.

But tonight was a night for celebration and the place was Amrhein's, a popular restaurant on West Broadway in South Boston that had been around since 1890. Located at the bottom of a four-story brick building (tenants lived above it), it was a popular watering hole for politicians the likes of former Mayor James Michael Curley and the current Mayor, the Honorable John F. Collins, as well as an assortment of city councilors, selectman, democrats, republicans, and various other political persuasions.

Liam and some of his fellow newly-minted firefighters were seated around a large round table strewn with beer bottles and bowls of potato chips and pretzels. One of the men, Joey Saniuk, had just returned from the restaurant's long oak bar with six beer bottles in his two large hands. After clinking their bottles, the men toasted each other and laughed. An Irish fiddle tune rang out from a nearby jukebox.

Now on his seventh or eighth Schlitz, Liam got unsteadily to his feet and told his companions he had to "drain the vein," which everyone thought was hilarious (it seemed that the "funny joke bar" is set very low when you drink a lot). Laughing along with everyone else, Liam worked his way through the crowd, side-stepped a waitress carrying a tray full of food, and made his way to the men's room. He opened the wooden door and walked in to do his business.

While standing at the urinal, his eyes closed and head swaying slightly to the music he could still hear coming from the dining room, Liam didn't notice that someone had entered the bathroom and was washing his hands at the sink, that was until her heard his name.

"Hello, Liam. Haven't seen you in, what, some 15 years. How have ya been, boyo?"

Liam zipped up and looked at the man washing his hands. It took a moment for his soggy brain to conjure up an image, but soon the fog cleared and that horrible day in 1942 suddenly emerged. The man was much older looking now, but there was no mistaking who he was.

"Hello, Mr. Fitzroy," Liam said. "Surprised to see you here."

"I don't know why, bucko," he said with a chuckle. "I own half the joint."

Liam wasn't surprised; Danny "Fitzy" Fitzroy was still the kingpin on the South Boston streets, and he still had his hands in everything.

Fitzroy took a paper towel from a dispenser and started to wipe his hands. "So you're going to be a fireman, huh?"

"That's right."

"Seems a bit poetic, don't you think?" He tossed the balled-up paper towel in a bucket. "Considering what went down that night."

Liam felt himself start to anger, but fought to keep it under control. Instead he asked, "How's Conor?"

"Oh, the boy is taking a little vacation over in the motherland with my brother. You know, just until things cool down a little more." Then Fitzroy looked hard at Liam, who felt himself take a step back; even at 60 years old, Fitzroy was still a formidable presence.

"By the way, I saw your mum last Sunday in Church. She's looking good, healthy-like. I can't imagine how it would kill her if her son ended up in Walpole as an accessory to murder."

Liam felt his face redden and fists clench. Fitzroy walked over and patted him gently on the cheek. "Good luck with the new job," Fitzroy said. "I'll give Conor your best when I hear from him next." And with that the gangster grinned and walked out leaving Liam fuming as he leaned forward and clenched the sides of the porcelain sink. If he could have he would have ripped it from the wall.

* * * * *

Now driving the Mass Turnpike out to Framingham, Liam turned up the volume on his 8-track player and sang along with Don McLean's "American Pie." He had hoped he'd never have a reason to be in the same room with Fitzroy again but now that seemed unlikely.

Fitzroy had held his own as the kingpin in South Boston for nearly 30 years, while taking the time to bury quite a few bodies in those three decades. But when you're the leader of the pack there's always a bigger and badder someone lurking behind you, and in 1965 that person lurking was one James "Whitey" Bulger, who was some 35 years younger than Fitzroy. Bulger had just been released from Alcatraz where he was serving time for bank robbery, and he was now anxious to carve out a name for himself. The strategy made sense as Bulger had the backing of Somerville mobster Howie Winter, head of the Winter Hill Gang. At first, Fitzroy tried to hold Bulger at bay, but in 1969 Fitzroy barely escaped death when his car was blown-up on Causeway Street as he was leaving a Celtics game at the Boston Garden, reportedly by one of Bulger's lieutenants. At that point, Fitzroy agreed to go quietly into the sunset. But it wasn't a happy retirement; in 1970 Fitzroy suffered a stroke that paralyzed his left side. He currently resides in an assisted care facility in Framingham, about 20 miles west of the Irish neighborhood he once ruled with an iron fist and where Liam was now heading and hoping to get some answers.

Liam pulled his car into an empty space at the front entrance of the Sunset Lake Assisted Care Center, a three-story red-brick building across the street from Lake Cochituate. Entering the large foyer, he smiled at a pretty girl who was manning the front desk and said hello. She had her head down reading what Liam could see was a copy of *Jonathan Livingston Seagull*. When she heard Liam's voice she looked up and returned the smile. She had long blonde hair and what looked like a sunflower painted on her left cheek. Large hoop earrings hung from each ear.

"Hi, can I help you?"

"Yes, please. I'm here to see this resident." Liam slid a piece of paper across the desk. "I made arrangements earlier with the Director."

The young girl read the name on the slip of paper and her brow wrinkled for a moment. She looked back at Liam with some confusion on her face.

"This is who you want to talk to?"

Liam nodded. "Yes... please."

She looked at the name once more. Her smile returned.

"Okay, please follow me."

She led Liam down a long hallway, past numerous closed doors where various sounds escaped; voices yelling for medication, voices yelling into telephones, voices screaming out the answers while watching *The Price is Right*.

They stopped just outside a door with the number 1215 on it. The young girl looked at Liam. "Should I say you're here?"

Liam shook his head and smiled once again. "No, no, that's fine… I'd like to surprise him."

"Umm, okay…that's cool. I hope you enjoy your visit. Peace." Then she went back towards her desk. Liam watched her walk down the hall, her mini-skirt swaying left to right, and when she was out of sight, he looked once more at the door, took a deep breath, and opened it.

The room was dimly lit and smelled like disinfectant and old age. But even in the low light Liam could make out a figure in a wheelchair sitting and gazing out the window.

"Did you bring my medicine?" a voice growled, sounding raspy and weather-beaten, plus it also seemed oddly muffled. When Liam didn't answer, the man turned his chair around and started to push it slowly forward. "What are ya fuckin' deaf! I said..." But when he saw it wasn't a nurse standing there he stopped.

It had been 16 years since Liam had laid eyes on Danny "Fitzy" Fitzroy. Of course, he had read accounts in *The Boston Globe* about his battles with Bulger and his stroke, but he wasn't prepared for what was in front of him. The once formidable gangster was now no more than a withered shell sitting in a chair. His body seemed to have caved in on him, his left arm hung uselessly at his side, and an oxygen mask covered the lower half of his face. Most of his hair was gone and dark brown age spots dotted his head. Liam watched him take a pair of glasses from his pocket with his one good hand and struggle to put them on. When he did, he squinted at Liam, who almost felt pity for him. *Almost.*

It took a moment, but the memory file cabinet in Fitzroy's withered brain still contained a few drawers that opened, and he glared at the man standing in front of him.

"Mulvaney! What the hell do you want?"

"What I *don't* want is to be in the same room with you, you pathetic piece of shit," Liam said. "What I *do* want is to know if your psycho son is back and if he's the one setting fires and killing people."

Liam wasn't prepared for the reaction he received. Anticipating a verbal onslaught, Liam was surprised to see Fitzroy exhale in resignation, his shoulders slumping. He used his good right arm to pull his left arm up onto his lap.

"He came back last April."

"Why?"

"There was a fire; killed my brother. Police out there weren't sure how it started."

115

"Conor?"

"I dunno… maybe."

Liam waited for Fitzroy to continue.

"After what happened at the Cocoanut Grove, the police were sure to start to put the pieces together, figuring the fire and the bank heist happening at the same time was too coincidental. To be on the safe side I shipped him out to my brother's place near Galway. Conor wasn't happy about it. We had words."

"Go on."

"He was always a loose cannon," Fitzroy continued, sucking more heavily through his oxygen mask. "There was never supposed to be people dying that night; all I told him was to create some smoke, get the cops heading over there. He took it too far."

Liam felt the anger rising inside him.

"So, you knew these fires were being set by Conor and that people were dying—women and children were dying—and you said *nothing* to the police!"

The old man sobbed. "I couldn't; he's my son!"

Liam stared at the pathetic sight in front of him and then turned to leave.

"What are you going to do?"

Liam paused, his hand on the door knob. "I'm going to stop him and put him away for the rest of his life. He can rot in prison."

Suddenly the old Fitzroy emerged from the withered shell and he screamed at Liam's back.

"You can't do that! He's my son! If you do this I will let the world know that YOU made him what he is!"

Liam turned. He looked at the man heaving in his chair; Fitzroy's breathing coming so fast his oxygen mask was fogged, the face now turning blood-red.

"I'll kill you!" he screamed, rising from his chair, only to collapse on the floor. Liam looked down at him and then turned to leave. Shouts of "I'll kill you" now muffled behind the closed door as Liam walked down the hallway to the front desk. The woman looked up from her book and smiled.

"How was your visit?"

"Oh, it was grand," Liam answered. "But when you get a chance you should maybe check on him; I think he's having a heart attack."

The girl looked horrified. The smile never left Liam's face.

"But take your time, really, finish your book. I've read it and it's very good." And with that Liam turned and left the building.

Chapter Eleven

Boston... Monday, August 28, 1972

BOSTON HERALD TRAVELER
AND
Record American

PARTLY CLOUDY

LATE CITY
Complete

THE WEATHER: PARTLY CLOUDY, WARM   MONDAY, AUGUST 28, 1972   44 PAGES   FIFTEEN CENTS

A Message From the Publisher

CITY ON FIRE!

Firebug Terrorizes

Boston; 64 Dead

HAROLD G. KERN
PUBLISHER

RESTON

Fear held the city in a vice-like grip. As a major tourist destination, the summer in Boston is usually thriving; theatres are full, restaurants are packed, museums draw large crowds. But the fires had put a major crimp in the summer, as people were hesitant to be in public places, particularly enclosed areas (Fenway Park, however, was still packing in the fans although the team was just so-so).

The front page of the *Boston Herald Traveler* and its glaring headline was lying on Captain Jo-Jo Calvino's desk and he was standing behind it, staring down while leaning forward on two massive fists. His face was red and several veins stuck out on his bald head. His breath came in short spurts. Liam Mulvaney and Terry Tillman sat in his office, poised for the explosion they knew was imminent. Yesterday Liam succumbed and showed the messages that had been aimed at him to his Captain, who in turn produced them in a meeting this morning with Mayor Kevin White and Police Superintendent Robert Bradley. Needless to say, that didn't go over too well.

Although Liam had turned over the messages (making sure to keep copies for himself), he didn't divulge to his superior his suspicions on who the firebug was, as that would raise too many questions on why Liam even suspected Conor Fitzroy as the perpetrator in the first place. And at this point even Tillman didn't know; although Liam felt eventually he would have to confide in him. Besides, maybe Tillman could help him figure out what the messages meant, because Liam had to admit he didn't have a clue.

Calvino stood up and turned around so his back was facing Liam and Tillman. He bent over slightly at the waist with his buttocks protruding. Without looking back he put his hand around and pointed at his backside.

"Are my pants all ripped?"

Liam and Tillman looked at each other. Tillman shrugged. "Excuse me, sir?" he said.

"I said... are my pants ripped to shreds?" Calvino's voice raised a notch. "They must be, because less than three hours ago the Mayor and that asshole Bradley... *CHEWED MY ASS OUT!*"

Calvino turned around and sat heavily into his chair, which groaned and creaked under his immense girth. He stared hard at Liam and pointed one of his fat fingers in his direction. "And you, you Irish fuck, they both wanted to throw you in jail for obstructing justice!"

"I'm sorry," was all Liam could think to say.

"And, do you know why you're not now playing hide the soap at MCI-Walpole, Mulvaney?" Liam thought it prudent not to answer. "It's because I convinced his holiness the Mayor that you had some unique insight on how we can stop this maniac, since he was directing messages at you for some strange reason. Would you say that's an accurate assumption, Mulvaney?"

Liam shifted in his chair slightly. "Umm, yes, sir. I do have some... theories."

Calvino looked at Tillman, who was hoping the Captain had forgotten he was in the room. "And you... you better hope your partner finds out who is doing this and what his end game is, or I will personally see that *you* get shipped back to Bumfuck, Louisiana!"

"Actually, sir, it's Missi..." Calvino's glare stopped him in his tracks. "I mean, yes sir."

Calvino angrily balled up the newspaper and threw it in a trash basket next to his desk. "Both of you get the hell out of here," he roared. "Do your job!"

While Liam Mulvaney and Terry Tillman were getting their respective asses chewed out, over on Morrissey Boulevard Robbie Bernstein was hard at work in the *Globe's* offices interviewing survivors from the Cocoanut Grove fire. The week before he had put out word in the paper looking for survivors who would like to discuss the event, as background information for the article the Spotlight Team was working on. Robbie had hoped that by doing so he might get more insight into what really happened that tragic night, the night his sister perished.

There had been quite a few responses and Robbie had matched them up to the employee records they had acquired; hat check girls, cooks, waiters, all with harrowing tales to tell about that fateful night. Some had even broken down and cried while recounting that horrible evening; the memory still raw. And with each story he thought of his sister, Peggy, and he had to keep himself from choking up.

Robbie was now about to start his last interview of the day. The person sitting across the table from him said his name was Carl Lumley. From what Robbie could see, Mr. Lumley was about 50 years of age and overweight, his stomach pushing into the table in front of him. He had brown-grey hair that looked like a bad comb-over, thick dark-framed glasses and a small thin mustache. He smiled nervously. Robbie looked over the sheet in front of him.

"Thank you for coming in, Mr. Lumley," Robbie said, staring down at the sheet. "For some reason I don't see your name on the list of employees on duty that night."

"Oh, that's easy to explain," Lumley said pleasantly. "You see, I'm a trumpet player and at the last minute the regular guy couldn't make it so they reached out to me to fill in for him."

"I see." At this point Robbie was tired and he just wanted the last interview done so he could go home, so he didn't question the explanation, which seemed perfectly plausible.

"So you were there that night," Robbie said. "And excuse me for sounding insensitive, but can I assume the burns on your face are a result of the fire?"

Lumley touched the left side of his face. "Sadly, yes," he said. "But I was a lot luckier than a lot of people." Robbie thought briefly of Peggy, a then moved forward.

"Was there anything that struck you as odd that night?"

"Odd?"

"I realize the fire sticks out in your mind the most, but was there anything else that night that you remember? Something that has stuck with you all this time."

Lumley gave the impression he was thinking hard.

"You know, Mr. Bernstein," Lumley said. "There was something that did seem a little… *unusual*."

"Oh?"

"Well, about 9 p.m. we had taken a break and I needed to use the restroom. I remember we just ended with a killer rendition of 'Chattanooga Choo Choo', if I do say so myself. Do you mind if I smoke?"

Robbie pushed an ashtray across the table. Lumley smiled and took out a pack of cigarettes. He put a cigarette in his mouth and patted his jacket. He looked at Robbie. "I seemed have lost my lighter. Do you have a light?"

Robbie took out his own lighter and lit the cigarette for him. Lumley took a deep puff and continued.

"So after the number I went downstairs and while I was walking around, I saw this worker, maybe a bus boy, I'm not sure, open up a door that was locked, a door leading out to a back alley."

Robbie sat up a little straighter in his chair. "And why did that seem strange, Mr. Lumley?"

"I thought it was strange because that door, from what I had heard, was always locked."

"But this person, maybe a bus boy, he unlocked it?'

Lumley nodded. "And after he did he held it open and this really scary guy walked in. Trust me, not someone I'd want to run into in a dark alley, no sirree. He was kind of like a thug, or a gangster-type, you know?"

Robbie quickly scribbled some notes. "Did you happen to hear anything they said to each other?"

"Well, yes, as a matter of fact I did," Lumley said. "This guy, he patted the kid on the cheek and I heard him say, *'Good lad, Liam, now get the fuck out of here; I got work to do.'* Excuse my language."

Robbie couldn't believe what he was hearing. He thought he felt his hand shake as he scratched two thick red lines under Liam Mulvaney's name on his sheet. Carl Lumley smiled.

Chapter Twelve

Wednesday, September 13, 1972

It was mid-September and sadly many of the city's planned post-Labor Day weekend activities had been cancelled. Over the past few weeks many restaurants were serving only half the amount of customers they normally would in August and September, while many movie houses simply chose to shut down. Tourism was taking a hit as well. Boston was now starting to feel the economic pain.

Liam Mulvaney sat in his office. The good news was that there hadn't been any more fires since Captain Calvino ripped into him and Tillman, but neither was he ready to divulge what he knew about Conor Fitzroy as a possible suspect, especially where he had no real hard evidence. But by withholding what he *did* know from the authorities, was he putting lives in jeopardy?

Before Liam could answer his own question, Jerry Sinclair yelled over to him from a desk up the front.

"Mulvaney, guy on the phone wants to talk with you."

"Who is it?"

"Wouldn't say; says you know him."

"Do I owe him money?"

"Don't know. But knowing you; yeah, probably."

"Smart ass; put him through."

A few seconds later the phone rang on Liam's desk. "Mulvaney," he said, trying not to sound bored. But when he heard the voice on the other line, boredom was no longer an issue.

"Hello, boyo. It's been awhile."

Liam felt his blood chill. "Conor."

"Ah, you remember me. That's good. We have so much to catch up on."

Liam felt he had to choose his words carefully. "Why are you doing this?"

"What, these little disturbances?" Conor laughed. "Why, they're just appetizers for the main course; just to get your attention."

"And the notes you've been leaving me. What the hell do they mean?"

Another laugh. "Don't think of them as messages, boyo, think of them as… a roadmap."

"A roadmap to where?"

"Now what fun would that be?"

"You know that I could tell the police who you are."

There was a moment of silence on the line. "True, you could," Conor finally said. "But then, who knows, maybe we wind up in neighboring cells once it's found out how you were involved in all the fun back in '42. Or your mum has an accident. And, besides," Conor continued. "You may be getting a call from your friend at the *Globe* very soon, wanting to talk more about that fun time we had back then."

Liam felt his hand gripping the phone. "What are you talking about?"

A chuckle. "Seems Mr. Bernstein interviewed Carl Lumley about that night, and your name came up."

Liam wracked his brain trying to remember the name, but came up blank. "I don't know any Carl Lumley."

"No matter, he knew a lot about you," Conor said, and Liam could hear him giggle. "Let's just say Mr. Lumley had first-hand knowledge of the events that went on that night."

Liam felt like his head was in a fog, unsure of what to say next. But before he could respond, Conor threw another log on a fire that was starting to burn out of control.

"Oh, by the way, I heard you visited my dear old da in Framingham, but he wouldn't tell you where I was."

"Yeah, it was hard to believe he would protect such a monster." Liam felt his anger start to rise. "I was surprised how much he still loves you."

"*STILL LOVES ME!* That's a joke," Conor shouted into the phone, forcing Liam to hold the phone back from his ear. "That shite ruined my life! I did everything he wanted me to do that night and what thanks do I get; he ships me off to his feckin' brother over in Ireland! Ships me out like some kind of a FedEx package!" Liam could hear heavy breathing, but when Conor returned on the line his voice was calm and steady. "But those days have come and gone, boyo. The old man is where he deserves to be... in hell."

Liam tried to compose his thoughts. "What are you talking about?"

"What's the matter, Liam… don't you watch the news?" And with that Conor disconnected the call.

Liam put the phone slowly back on the cradle. Then it dawned on him. "Jerry," he yelled. "Put on the news…" But when he looked up he could see that Jerry Sinclair was leaning against his desk already watching the news report. Liam walked over beside him and his stomach fell as the graphic showed the Sunset Lake Assisted Care Center fully engulfed in flames, as Terry Carter, a reporter for Channel 4, gave his report.

Reporter: "The fire broke out around 9 a.m., reportedly starting in the basement. It quickly spread to the first floor where many of the residents resided. Because of the fast-moving flames, much of the building was consumed before firefighters arrived. At this moment they are reporting at least five fatalities, four of them residents, the most notable being Daniel Fitzroy, a longtime underworld figure in South Boston."

News Anchor back at the studio: "Terry, you mentioned five fatalities, of which four were residents."

Reporter: "That's right, Jack, sadly the fifth was a young woman who worked at the front desk; Emily Barrett, age 19 from Natick, Framingham Police are treating the incident as possible arson. Back to you, Jack."

Liam couldn't listen anymore so he slowly walked back to his desk. Once there he took out the copies he had made of the messages Conor had left him, thinking this was the only way he was going to stop this psychopath. He started to reach for the phone to call Tillman, who had the day off, but before he could pick up the receiver he heard Jerry yell his name.

"Mulvaney, Robbie Bernstein from the *Globe* on line 2."

Liam thought for a moment. Finally he told Jerry to take a message. He needed to put off a face-to-face with Bernstein as long as possible. But he did feel like the walls were starting to close in.

Chapter Thirteen

Boston... Thursday, October 5, 1972

The week before Columbus Day weekend usually finds Boston bursting at the seams as hundreds of thousands of college students have already descended on the city like hungry locusts.

Located in Boston's Back Bay section, Emerson College falls into that category. Although not as big as its counterparts—Boston University and Boston College—just to name a few, it is an institution of higher learning that continues to grow in stature.

Founded in 1880 by Charles Wesley Emerson as a "School of Oratory," it become renowned for its advancements in teaching communications, with the FCC awarding the college a 10-watt license in 1949, and WERS, the first educational FM radio station in New England, was born. The station's power was increased to 300 watts three years later and 18,000 watts by 1953.

As the 1960s started, Emerson College became more attractive to out-of-state students when a building it owned at 373 Commonwealth Avenue was sold and the proceeds were used to buy another building at 100 Beacon Street earmarked to house dormitories. In 1964, Emerson College, ever expanding, purchased two additional buildings: 96 Beacon Street, which became the student union building, and 132–134 Beacon Street, which became a dormitory, and was now the home for the next four years for a very excited freshman from Albany, New York.

Smiling from ear to ear, 18-year old Chris Pikula couldn't believe how lucky he was to get accepted to Emerson College. While his high school classmates back home only concentrated on sports, cars and girls, Chris always had a love for TV news broadcasting, and would spend hours in his room at home using a ruler for a microphone and making believe he was broadcasting some huge event (*"That's right, Melanie. I'm standing on the runway at JFK airport and The Beatles have just landed!").* Chris knew Emerson had its own broadcast station and he was pumped to be involved.

Chris' dorm was a five-story brownstone typical of Boston's Back Bay, located right on the corner of Berkeley Street and not too far from the Charles River. The living area was on the upper floors and the bottom floor was the location of the Phi Omega Xi fraternity, probably the coolest fraternity on campus. And as tradition had dictated over the years, the upper classmen, who were most of the members of the fraternity, every Columbus Day weekend invited the incoming freshmen to party with them.

Chris and his new roommate, Jon Lee, who was actually from Taiwan, arrived just before 8 p.m. and the fraternity was in full party mode. Cream's "Sunshine of Your Love" was blaring from two huge speakers set up on both sides of a stereo system, black light posters gave off an eerie glow, several girls in short skirts and wearing beads were swaying on a make-shift dance floor, and the sweet smell of marijuana wafted about the room.

"This is s-o-o-o- cool," was all Chris could think to say. But Jon was too busy watching the girls dance, a goofy smile on his face. Before Chris could say more, a huge beefy arm fell on his shoulder, connected to one of the biggest guys he'd ever seen.

"Jimmy Burns, class of '74," the hulk said. "Welcome to Phi Omega Xi!" Chris would have guessed if Emerson had a football team, Jimmy Burns would be the star linebacker.

"Chris Pikula... ah, class of 1976," he said. "This is my roommate, Jon Lee." Chris elbowed Jon in the back, drawing his attention away from the dancers.

"What?" said an annoyed Jon. Then he saw who Chris was talking to. "Whoa!"

"Well, dudes," Jimmy said. "There's a tradition at Phi Omega Xi that when the beer runs out, the freshmen go get more."

"Um, okay," Chris answered. "Where, um, do we get it?"

"Good question," Jimmy replied with a big smile on his face. He now had both Chris and Jon under each large arm and was walking them towards the back of the room.

"We keep the kegs in the basement," Jimmy said, pointing at a door. "You'll probably need both of you to carry one; they're kind of heavy."

"Sure," Chris said. "C'mon Jon, let's do this."

"Groovy, man," Jimmy said. "I'll be right here waiting for you. Hurry up, people are thirsty!"

Wooden stairs led down to a basement, which Chris and Jon carefully navigated as a single bulb seemed to be the only light source, except for some dirty basement windows allowing some of the street lights in.

"This place gives me the creeps," Jon said, and then he jumped when an old boiler fired up. "Jesus Christ!"

"Keep walking; the beer must be somewhere in the back," Chris said, trying to keep the nervousness out of his voice. Suddenly the heard a sound, like metal containers being moved around.

"What was that?" Jon asked with a shaky voice. Above their heads they could hear the thumping bass of a song that Chris thought sounded vaguely familiar (*The Who?*).

Chris didn't answer, but he stopped when he saw ahead of him a shadow that looked like a man hovering over some containers. Chris figured maybe he was one of the school's custodians; and perhaps he knew where they kept the kegs of beer. As both boys ventured forward to ask their question, they immediately noticed that the containers were red gasoline cans, and that the man, who Chris could see more clearly now, was pouring its contents into a corner; both on the floor and on the walls. The smell of gasoline was getting stronger and stronger.

"Ah, excuse me," Chris said. "Could you..." Upon hearing Chris, the man, who was hunched over, turned and faced the two boys, who immediately stepped back when they saw the man was wearing a gasmask. Before Chris and Jon could comprehend what was happening, the man moved quickly towards them. As he did he grabbed a two-foot metal bar from a stack of boxes and swung it viciously, connecting with Jon's head before he could even move. Chris gasped and fell against a wall, staring at his new roommate lying in a pool of blood. Chris then looked over at the man breathing heavy in the gasmask, just as his own life was snuffed out before even giving his first newscast on WERS.

The ensuing fire could have been more catastrophic if a passerby walking his dog behind the building around 8:30 p.m. had not seen flames coming out of the basement window and ran to a pay phone to call 911. Still, even with a rapid response from the firehouse on Boylston Street, much of the first floor had been consumed in the flames coming up from the basement.

It was just after 1 a.m. when Liam and Tillman arrived at the site. The Fire Marshall, Trent Gibbons, was on site when they arrived and was instructing some of his men on what to do next. He walked over when he saw Liam and Tillman looking at the building from the sidewalk. Police had cordoned off the area with sawhorses with BPD stenciled on them in black paint. Several police cars with their lights flashing gave the building an eerie blue glow.

Anticipating their questions, Gibbons told them what he knew. "It's believed the fire broke out in the basement around 8:30 p.m.; called in by a passerby.

That caught Liam's attention. "Did he see anybody in the area?"

Gibbons looked at his notes. "Says he saw a guy, maybe middle-aged. White. Carrying something in his hand. Walking very fast."

"Anything else?"

Gibbons turned a page. "Yeah, when the guy passed under a street light the witness said it looked like the side of his face was all scarred and purple."

"Like a burn?"

"Maybe." Gibbons continued his report. "Anyway, flames shot up through the floor where one of those fraternity parties was underway, started a panic. Most got out; five didn't." Gibbons pointed up at the upper floors. "Good thing we contained it as quickly as we did because there are a hundred or so students living on those upper floors."

Tillman let out a low whistle. "Damn."

"One other thing," Gibbons added. "According to the medical examiner on the scene, from what he could see two of the deceased were in the basement, not on the first floor."

"Why in the basement?" Tillman asked.

Gibbons shook his head. "No clue. But from what the ME could see, the two in the basement likely didn't die in the fire." Liam turned and looked at the Fire Marshall.

"What do you mean?"

"From what he can tell it looks like their heads were bashed in."

Liam thought about that for a moment. "Maybe they came upon the perp."

Gibbons shrugged. "Could be. I assume you still want to walk the site?"

"If it's okay," Liam said.

Gibbons gestured towards the building. "Be my guest."

Liam and Tillman donned their protective gear and started forward. But Liam had only moved a few paces when they heard Gibbons yell his name.

"Hold up," he said. Gibbons walked over to his car and took an envelope from the front seat. "This was left on my windshield; had your name on it." He held out the envelope, but Liam made no move to take it; eyeing the envelope like it was a cobra ready to strike.

"Thanks," Tillman said, taking the envelope from the Fire Marshall. Gibbons looked at Liam for a moment, a strange look on his face, and then he touched the brim of his hat and headed back to his car. Once Gibbons was gone, Tillman opened the envelope and took out the piece of paper.

"Read it," Liam said.

Tillman did, and then handed it to Liam, who read once again out loud.

Do You Get Satisfaction For A Job Well Done?

Chapter Fourteen

Boston... Friday, October 20, 1972

Although frustrated that Liam Mulvaney has been dodging his phone calls, Robbie Bernstein was compelled to push on with his investigation on what really happened the night of the Cocoanut Grove fire in 1942. He also had to admit that *maybe* he also understood, to a point, the pressure Mulvaney must be under what with the fires that have been consuming the city. But Robbie had promised himself that he would still discover the truth of what happened the night his sister died, and in doing so determine whether or not Mulvaney had a part in it. And based on his interview with Carl Lumley, he was definitely leaning in that direction.

On the same night the Cocoanut Grove burned down in 1942, the First National Bank of Boston in Post Office Square was hit. Thieves broke through an adjacent wall and made off with $3.5 million. They took their time because every cop car in Boston was tied up in Park Square to tend to the dead and dying. Robbie Bernstein never believed in coincidences and he wasn't about to start now.

Going through the *Globe's* archives, Robbie tracked down the name of the FBI agent who was in charge of investigating the bank heist; Special Agent Gerald Geiger, currently retired from the Bureau and residing in Quincy. Robbie thought it best to give him a call and set up an interview in person.

Later that afternoon, Robbie Bernstein was sitting in the small living room of Special Agent Geiger, now 75-years old and pretty much permanently attached to an oxygen tank placed on the floor beside him as he sat on a worn-looking couch. Geiger saw Robbie eyeing the container.

"Way too many unfiltered Lucky's," Geiger said, his voice sandpaper raspy. "Doc said I probably won't live to see the Red Sox finally win a World Series." He laughed. "Not exactly going out on a limb since they haven't done it since Calvin Coolidge was President." He adjusted the nose clip that led to the oxygen tank. "So, what's on your mind? I assume you're not here trying to sell me a subscription to the *Globe*."

"Actually, Special Agent Geiger…"

"Jerry will do; that was a long time ago."

"Jerry… I wanted to talk about the First National Bank robbery on November 28, 1942."

"The night of the Cocoanut Grove fire."

Robbie nodded; he was continually surprised by how many people knew that date. Geiger eyed him, and then a smile appeared.

"You think there was a connection, don't you?" he said.

Robbie shrugged. "I don't know; maybe."

Geiger took the nose-clip out and placed it on the couch beside him. He then proceeded to light up a cigarette and take a deep drag. He blew the smoke into the air where it hung over

149

his head like a cloud. Robbie eyed the oxygen canister nervously but said nothing.

"You might be right," Geiger said. "Saturday night in the Post Office Square area and not a soul around; what are the odds? Everyone was either at the fire or home listening on the radio. Not many TV's back then. Not a cop to be found for miles."

Robbie jotted down a few notes. "Did you ever figure anyone for the job?" Robbie asked. Geiger laughed, which caused him to choke a little and lose his breath. He stubbed out the cigarette and put his oxygen back on. After taking a deep breath he continued.

"Sure we did; Danny Fitzroy was at the top of our list. He was making a name for himself in Southie back then; gambling, prostitution, running some drugs. It seemed to us that it was only a matter of time until he graduated to bank robbery. Hey, we can't let those Charlestown kids have all the fun, now can we?"

Geiger took another deep breath. "But, hey, payback's a bitch, right? Heard he checked out in a fire at some nursing home in Framingham where his sorry ass was living."

"What about his son?"

"Conor?" Geiger replied. "A piece of shit, just like his old man. I haven't heard his name recently. But if the father was involved, you can bet the kid was, too."

"Did the Bureau keep tabs on them after the robbery?"

"The father, yeah," Geiger answered. "The kid, not so much; fell off the grid right after the heist. There was talk he was living in Ireland. Good riddance to bad rubbish, that's how I see it."

Geiger removed the nosepiece and reached once again for his pack of cigarettes. Robbie decided not to press his luck a second time. He thanked Geiger for his help and said his goodbyes. As he was getting ready to leave, Geiger gave him one last parting piece of advice.

"If you ever *do* run into Conor Fitzroy, I advise you to head in the other direction," he said. "Because Conor Fitzroy is one mean motor scooter."

The Story of Conor Timothy Fitzroy

Although his father only wanted Conor to put together a distraction at the Cocoanut Grove in 1942—a little smoke, maybe a small fire in the basement—Conor took his job seriously. He had always loved the look of fire, its heat and power, ever since as a kid when he sprayed a neighbor's cat with lighter fluid and set it on fire, laughing as it ran away.

Unfortunately, once inside the club, Conor let his imagination run wild and he set off numerous fires in several storage areas, many being used as storage for paper goods and decorations. But even Conor was unprepared for what happened next as the old club was a virtual tinderbox and it only took minutes for the walls and ceiling to be engulfed in flames. Conor suddenly found himself in the middle of the catastrophe he had started. He raced for the door he entered in from and just before reaching it a fiery beam came down and hit him on the side of his face, knocking him to the floor. He cried out in pain as the red-hot timber burned his flesh. Finally, he made it to the door, got out and ran down the alley where a car had been waiting, listening to the screams of the club's patrons as he ran.

The next day, instead of being concerned with his son's scarred face, "Fitzy" Fitzroy was livid. He screamed at Conor that it was only supposed to be a diversion, not a mass murder. He said the cops are going to start making the connection and once they see his son suffered burns on the same night the Cocoanut Grove burned to the ground, it would raise suspicion. Therefore, despite Conor's protests, his father sent him off to Ireland to live with his brother in Rosmuc, a small village about 20 miles west of Galway.

Conor lived with Ian Fitzroy and his wife for nearly 20 years and hated every minute of it. His Aunt Maureen was decent enough, although she carried the scars and bruises of a bad marriage. Ian Fitzroy was a mean drunk and he treated Conor like something he stepped in and couldn't wait to scrape off. He and Ian came to blows several times, with Conor usually taking the worst of it. But by 1962, Conor had enough and one night when Aunt Maureen was at a friend's house, he locked a very drunk Ian Fitzroy inside that small thatch-roofed cottage and burned it to the ground, laughing as flames licked the night sky.

Realizing it was probably time to leave Ireland, in 1964 Conor finally ended up in London, where he met Reggie and Ronnie Kray, two gangsters that were ruling London's underworld. The Krays didn't mind that the side of his face looked like purple oatmeal, they just appreciated the fact the Conor knew how to burn down a building, like the pub in Whitechapel where the owner refused to pay the Krays protection money.

As fate would have it, one night while reading the *London Daily Mirror,* he came upon a small story about a large fire in South Boston. Seeing his hometown mentioned, Conor read it carefully and was surprised to see the name Liam Mulvaney, who apparently had saved several of his fellow firefighters, but lost a part of his leg in doing so.

In 1968, the Krays were arrested at Flat 43, Braithwaite House in East London, home of their mother Violet and father

Charles who were on holiday in Suffolk at the time. It felt to Conor Fitzroy that maybe it was time to head back home. After all, there was still some unfinished business to be had with dear old dad.

After short and busy stays in New York City, including the burning of an Episcopalian Church in Queens and a variety store in Brighton Beach, Conor finally made it back to Massachusetts, where he began to plan out his final masterpiece.

It was while drinking a beer in the lobby of a Holiday Inn in Taunton in March of 1972, that he saw a news clip on TV. It was reporting on a fire at a social club in Jamaica Plain, and there being interviewed was his old friend Liam Mulvaney, who was now—to Conor's surprise and delight—a full-fledged Fire Investigator. How delicious, Conor thought to himself, as he downed his Budweiser. What fun!

Chapter Fifteen

Boston... Friday, October 27, 1972

October was starting to fade and after the talk he had with Special Agent Gerald Geiger of the FBI, Robbie Bernstein was more determined than ever to catch up with Liam about his possible involvement the night the Cocoanut Grove burned down and lives were lost. With the interview with Carl Lumley still fresh in his mind, Robbie decided to take the proverbial bull by the horns and go directly at Mulvaney by showing up at his home unannounced. But before Robbie could plan his sneak attack, another shoe dropped. And this one was close to home for Liam and Tillman.

Sitting in their office in Brighton, Liam and Tillman tried desperately to figure out what the notes meant that were left behind. Liam was sure who left them, but was still struggling with whether to let Tillman in on what he knew, or thought he knew. Liam had the notes spread out on his desk, but they might as well been reading hieroglyphics.

Tillman leaned back in his chair and crossed his arms. "I am so lost, man," he said, and Liam could hear the frustration in his voice; he felt the same way. After a few minutes, Liam said to his partner, "Tillman, there's something you should know…" But before he had a chance to continue, his phone rang. Liam picked it up and the voice on the other line made him sit up straight in his chair.

"Hey, boyo. You know, your buddy Superfly should be careful of the company he keeps," Conor said. "He's got a nice little house in Dorchester. Pity to see it burn down." Conor laughed as he hung up.

Tillman saw Liam staring at the receiver in his hand. "What's up?" he asked. Liam put the phone back on its cradle and looked at Tillman. "Where are Nina and Bessie right now?"

"I dunno, why you asking?"

"Just answer me," Liam said, almost shouting. That spooked Tillman. "Bessie is in school and Nina is at work. What the hell is going on?"

"Grab your coat," Liam said as he jumped out of his chair. He collected the notes and put them in his pocket "I'm driving."

Once they reached Tillman's street the fire engines were already there in front of his house. Liam pulled over in front and Tillman jumped out almost before the car stopped. "Oh God," he said as he watched his small detached garage burn. Firefighters were working at extinguishing the flames while at the same time trying to prevent those same flames from leaping to Tillman's house which was a mere 10 feet away. Just then a taxi pulled up and Nina jumped out, her hair tied in a kerchief. She ran to her husband who held her tightly.

"Terry, what happened?" she asked; her hand to her mouth.

Tillman eyed Liam and then kissed his wife on the head. "It's okay, honey... maybe just some paint caught fire. The house is fine."

"Meet me at Foley's at 7 p.m.," Liam said softly to Tillman, and he walked back to his car.

When Tillman arrived Liam was sitting in a corner booth at Foley's, a bar in the South End often frequented by cops and firemen. He was nursing a Coke. Tillman sat across from Liam. He didn't look happy. As a matter of fact, he looked truly pissed-off. But before he could say anything Liam asked, "How's Nina?" And that served to defuse the situation a bit.

"She's fine," Tillman said, letting out a deep breath. "Just a little shook up." The waitress came over and Tillman ordered a Budweiser on draft. She smiled and went to fill the order. Once she left, Liam began.

"That call I got at the office was warning me—well actually you—that you should be careful of the company you keep; which would be me."

"And that voice also said my house was going to be torched?"

"It was implied."

Tillman gave Liam a hard stare, his eyes narrowing. "It was the same person who's been lighting the fires and leaving the notes, wasn't it?"

"Yes," Liam said, pausing to take a drink of his Coke. "His name is Conor Fitzroy."

Tillman looked confused; the name didn't resonate with him. "Who is that, and why does he have such a strong interest in you?"

"Do you recall the fire at the assisted living center in Framingham?"

"Yeah, the one where that gangster...." Tillman stopped. "Danny Fitzroy, the mob boss from your neck of the woods."

"Conor is his son," Liam said. "And Conor set that fire, killing his old man."

"So what's your connection with Conor?"

Liam took a deep breath, and then told only the third person in his life—after Father Doherty and Caleb—what happened in 1942. When he was finished, Tillman sat back, his eyes wide and not sure what to say.

Liam's head was bowed. "All those people," he said softly, and then he let out a sob.

Tillman regained his thoughts. "You were just a kid, man," he said, trying to inject some comfort.

Liam looked up at him, his eyes red. "One of the people who died that night was Peggy Regan," Liam said. "We were supposed to go out on a date a few days later."

"Man, that's tough," Tillman said.

"Oh, it's worse than that."

"How so?"

"You probably saw in the *Globe* that reporter whose been doing some stories on the Cocoanut Grove fire."

161

Tillman thought for a moment. "Yeah, Robbie something."

"Bernstein," Liam said. "Robbie Bernstein. He's been interviewing survivors of the fire to try and piece together what really happened that night. He's working on a huge investigative piece with the *Globe's* Spotlight Team."

"And you're afraid he's going to discover that you were involved?"

Liam shook his head and crunched some ice from his drink between his teeth. "No, I'm afraid he's going to find out I killed his sister."

"Excuse me?"

* * * * *

It was just after 9 p.m. when Liam pulled his car in front of his South Boston apartment. After making sure it was locked, Liam walked up to his steps but suddenly stopped when he saw who was sitting there.

"Mulvaney, we have to talk," Robbie Bernstein said.

Liam's shoulders slumped. "Sure, why not," he said as he started up the steps. "This seems to be the night for talking. C'mon in, I'll put coffee on."

Liam and Robbie sat across from each other, a long coffee table between them. Liam stared at the tape recorder. Somehow he knew this day might come. Robbie hit RECORD.

"Thanks for agreeing to speak with me," Robbie said.

Liam grinned. "Call me Liam. Didn't seem like I had much of a choice; unless you were planning to sleep on my stoop." Robbie smiled.

"Listen Mulvaney—Liam—I am aware that you are up to your neck in what's going on," Robbie explained. "But I have a job to do, just as you do."

Liam's eye shifted to the tape recorder, sitting there like some predatory beast waiting to chew him up and spit him out. He looked back at Robbie. "Go ahead. It's been a long day."

Robbie shuffled through some pages in his notebook. He came to the one he was looking for and looked up at Liam. He tapped the page with his finger.

"Before we talk about the Cocoanut Grove," Robbie said. "Were you aware that there was a large bank robbery across town the same night of the fire?"

This was not the opening question Liam expected, so it caught him off-guard. "I think so... maybe? Why do you ask?"

"Later," was all Robbie said. He turned another page in his notebook and continued after taking a sip of his coffee. "Pretty good; instant Sanka?"

"The espresso machine was broken." That brought a smile to Robbie's face. "Look," said Liam with some frustration. "Can we just get on with this? It feels like we're pulling a band-aid off a little at a time."

Robbie plowed ahead. "As you know, we're doing a Spotlight piece on what really happened the night of the Cocoanut Grove fire."

"And you don't believe it was just an accident?"

"No, I don't," Robbie said quickly. "I have interviewed a number of survivors from that night and they all said it was horrible but none could put their finger on what might have caused it. That is until I interviewed Carl Lumley."

The name meant nothing to Liam but he let Robbie continue.

"Now Mr. Lumley remembers you that night, and he had some interesting things to say."

"I don't remember any Carl Lumley working at the Cocoanut Grove."

"He wasn't an employee; he was in the band. Played the trumpet."

"I knew everyone in the band. And there was no brass; just guitars and drum."

Robbie was starting to get frazzled. The interview was getting off track and he needed to pull it back in.

"Lumley said he saw you open a back door around 9 p.m. and let somebody in; said the guy looked like a gangster. Is that true?"

Liam's mind was racing. "What did this Lumley look like?"

"Just answer the question."

"I will, I promise," Liam said. "Please, *what did he look like*?" He waited for Robbie to answer.

"Maybe 50 years old, kind of big, and he had…"

"Burns on the left side of his face," Liam interrupted. Robbie's jaw dropped.

"How did… you said you didn't know Carl Lumley."

Liam sat back in his chair. "There is no Carl Lumley," Liam said. "That was Conor Fitzroy. And everything he told you was true, except the part about who he was. That was just Conor playing mind games. He's a sociopath; you wouldn't believe some of the things I saw him do when we were kids."

Robbie was now totally confused. "I don't understand."

Liam took a deep breath. It was time to dive into the deep end of the confessional waters.

"The morning of the Grove fire I was summoned to meet with Fitzy Fitzroy and Conor at a small café he owned on West Broadway. I thought they were going to kill me."

"For what reason?"

"I really didn't think they needed a reason," Liam answered truthfully. "I couldn't figure out why they wanted to talk to me. Anyway, they mentioned me working at the Cocoanut Grove and for whatever reason they needed to create a small distraction to pull the cops away from something they had planned."

"The bank job," Robbie interjected.

"I didn't know it at the time, or maybe I thought it, but yeah, now it makes sense. They offered me $100, which for me and my mom was like $100 million at the time, and all I had to do was let Conor in the back door at 9 p.m." Liam paused. He could see Robbie starting to breathe a little heavier. But he continued.

"I had no idea what was going to happen," Liam stressed. "You have to believe me."

Robbie looked down at his notebook on the table. His response came through gritted teeth. "Over 450 people died that night. You have to own that. You know that, right?"

Liam nodded. "I do; I own it every day of my life. And now it's coming back at me in the worst way; Conor is killing people and making a game out of it."

But Robbie was still seething. "One of those people was my big sister."

"I was very fond of Peggy," Liam said. "She was a beautiful girl."

Robbie looked up; caught off guard. "You knew Peggy?"

Liam nodded. "We were supposed to go out on a date in the next few days."

"A date?"

Liam nodded again. "I'm sorry."

Robbie tried to compose himself by taking a few deep breaths. When he felt like he could control his emotions, he said, "You know I have to run this story. And when I do, your life is going to change, and not for the better. You might even end up in jail."

"I know," Liam said softly. "When is it running?"

"It's scheduled for Wednesday, November 29; a day after the 30th anniversary."

Liam let out a breath he felt like he was holding in for ages. He almost felt relieved. "Well, I have a job to do until then." Then an idea came to him. "Maybe you can help me with what's going on."

"Help you? With the fires?"

"Yes... I am going to tell you something pertinent to the fires; but it has to be off the record." Liam looked down at Robbie's tape recorder. No one moved for a few seconds. Then Robbie hit the STOP button.

Liam fished copies of the notes out of his pocket and spread them on the table. Robbie looked at them. "What do they mean?"

"That's just it," Liam said. "My people can't figure them out. The cops can't figure them out. But what I know is that Conor called them a roadmap to something big. Don't know what, don't know when." He paused to collect his thoughts. "My thinking is that maybe you're a fresh set of eyes, or maybe have access to data bases we don't through the *Globe*. But you can't tell anyone about these notes. Agreed?"

As Liam was talking, Robbie was carefully looking at each one, almost as if he wasn't listening to what Liam was saying. "Did you hear what I said?" Liam asked.

"Yes," Robbie said. "But I don't have to agree or disagree." Before a startled Liam could answer—now thinking maybe this was a huge mistake—Robbie took a pen out of his pocket. "Are these copies?" he asked.

"Yes," Liam answered. And with that Robbie took each note, underlined certain parts, and slid them back in front of Liam. He looked down at what Robbie had done.

Having fun? Ain't it <u>a gas, gas, gas.</u>

Could this be <u>the last time?</u>

I think what's puzzling you is the nature of my game.

Do you get satisfaction for a job well done?

The fire is sweeping our very streets today.

Liam stared hard at the notes. "What am I missing?"

"My wife is a huge Rolling Stones fan," Robbie said. "Sometimes I think that's all she plays on our stereo at home. She even got us tickets to one of their shows somewhere."

"Okay?"

Robbie picked up each note and explained what he underlined. "These are all either Rolling Stones song lyrics or song titles. 'Gas, gas, gas' is from the song 'Jumpin' Jack Flash'. 'The last time' is one of their songs. 'What's puzzling

172

you...' is from 'Sympathy for the Devil'. 'Satisfaction'... well, that's obvious. And the 'fire sweeping our streets' is a line taken from 'Gimme Shelter'."

Liam couldn't believe what he heard, but he was still at a loss. "So, what, Conor Fitzroy is a Rolling Stones fan... what does that mean? How does that help us?"

Robbie packed up his notes and tape recorder and stood to leave. "I don't know. But you still have work to do and I still have a story to write. Thanks for the coffee."

Liam watched Robbie leave, and as soon as he did he called Tillman. In his heart Liam wasn't sure he was any closer to stopping Conor, but at least he knew more today than he did yesterday.

Chapter Sixteen

Boston... Tuesday, November 7, 1972

Father Henry Doherty, now getting on in years, walked out of the Patrick F. Gavin School in South Boston and made his way through a forest of humanity holding up signs pushing their candidates for the 1972 Presidential Election. Being as he resided in a heavily Democratic state, Doherty was not surprised that most of the signs were pushing McGovern/Mondale, with a few outliers rallying for Nixon/Agnew. Doherty did his civic duty and was now heading back to Gate of Heaven Church on the other side of town. According to the national pollsters, they were predicting a landslide for Richard M. Nixon.

Doherty's knees were aching so he opted to forgo the bus and splurge on a taxi. Confessions started at 4 p.m. and he didn't want to be late. The church was empty when he walked in; not uncommon on a Tuesday afternoon, but he wanted to be available should any parishioner wish to confess their sins. Taking a brief moment to grab his purple liturgical vestments and drape them across his shoulders, he then entered the confessional and patiently waited, biding his time by reading the Gospel.

Ten minutes passed when the priest heard someone working the outside latch of his door. Figuring that person was unaware of which door to use, he directed them to the door beside his. He put away his Gospel when he thought the person had entered and was seated and slid the side door open; both parties now separated by just a lattice window.

"Bless me father for I have sinned," a man said in a soft voice. "It's been, maybe, I don't know; 30 years since my last confession."

"That's quite awhile, my son," Father Doherty said. "What are your sins?"

"Well, let's see," he said, "I've killed a lot of people, burned a lot of buildings, basically had a lot of fun."

The priest felt his body tense. "This is not a place to be joking," he said, his voice quivering a little. "I may have to ask you to leave." The man ignored him, his voice rising.

"So, Father, how many 'Hail Marys' and 'Our Fathers' do you think it will take to absolve my sins; 50, 100, maybe 500?"

Father Doherty started to slide the window closed, but stopped when the man mentioned someone he knew.

"What about Liam Mulvaney, Father? Did he tell you how many people he has killed? Did you absolve him of his sins?"

With this Father Doherty felt the strength needed to be indignant, "I don't discuss other people's confessions."

The man laughed and Father Doherty pushed on his door to leave but it wouldn't budge. He tried again harder, to no effect.

"You know, Father I bet you *did* clear his slate for what he did," the man said, and Father Doherty could hear him reaching under his jacket. "How about me? Am I forgiven? Didn't think so."

Before he could answer, Father Doherty suddenly felt his vestments being sprayed through the lattice window with what he immediately knew from the smell was lighter fluid. He tried to stand up in the confined space to get as far away from the spray as possible, but it continued to soak his clothes, floor and walls. Out of the corner of his eye he saw a yellow and orange flame flicker before his world turned to fire and pain.

The man casually exited his side of the confessional, ignoring the screams and smiling as smoke seeped up from under the door. He walked down the line of pews towards the large wooden doors leading out to the streets. He looked back briefly to see the entire confessional erupt into flames, now working their way towards the first row of wooden pews. With a final smile for a job well done, Conor Fitzroy dipped a finger in the holy water, blessed himself, and then exited the smoky church.

Liam rushed to the scene as soon as he heard the call, fully cognizant of whose parish it was. By the time he got there the fire was already well under control. Luckily, a parishioner had entered less than 15 minutes after Conor left and called it in. The structural damage was contained; both confessionals and the first two rows of pews were destroyed. The human loss; unimaginable.

Deputy Chief Chuck O'Hara was standing on the sidewalk when Liam pulled up, Liam knew from the look on his face there were casualties, and who that casualty was. O'Hara shook his head. "I'm sorry, Liam," O'Hara said solemnly. "We all loved him. No better man lived, and no man deserved to die like that."

Liam braced himself by leaning against a bus stop sign. He couldn't find any words to say. O'Hara spoke, "Before you ask, there was no message left for you at the scene."

Liam shook his head. "No, there was a message left, Chief, loud and clear," he said. "The message was: No one you love is safe."

Around 10 p.m. that night, Liam sat in his darkened apartment, trying to understand what was going on and how to stop it. He felt like the weight of the world was on his shoulders. His head was beginning to ache. He popped four

Tylenol; two more than the recommended dosage at one sitting. He closed his eyes and leaned back on the couch, waiting for the pain to subside.

"I'm not sure some pills are going to make everything magically go away," said the soft voice from across the room. Unsure if he heard something, Liam opened his eyes and recoiled at the sight in front of him. He closed his eyes hard and slowly reopened them, but nothing changed. Sitting in the same chair that Robbie sat in some nights before was his big sister Peggy, looking just like she had the last time Liam saw her. The only difference was this time the left side of her face was scarred and purple.

"We were supposed to go on a date, Liam," she said sweetly, smoothing out the lap of her blue dress. "Do you remember that?"

Liam nodded, not finding any words to say. Peggy smiled.

"Maybe we still can," she said smiling. She extended her hand. "Here, help me up, will you?"

Liam struggled slowly to his feet and took her hand. But then his false leg gave out and he fell back on the couch. And as he did the skin from Peggy's arm up to her elbow came with him, leaving nothing but bone. Liam screamed as loud as he could.

The pounding on his door woke him up. He was on his couch but his clothes were drenched in sweat.

"Mr. Mulvaney," the concerned voice on the other side of the door belonged to his neighbor, Mrs. Peterson. "Are you okay?" she shouted through the door. Liam tried to compose himself.

"Yes, yes, I'm fine," he said. "Just a bad dream."

"Okay," Mrs. Peterson said. "As long as you're fine."

But all Liam Mulvaney could think to himself was; I am *so* very far from being fine.

Chapter Seventeen

Boston... Thursday, November 23, 1972

Liam was more than content to spend Thanksgiving at the Toll House Inn in Whitman. The Toll House made history by inventing the toll house cookie in the 1930s and the restaurant had a charming traditional New England atmosphere and food. But Nina Tillman would not hear of it so she made her husband force Liam to do Thanksgiving at their house. He reluctantly agreed after Tillman said he couldn't return home unless he accepted. Besides, Bessie would be disappointed; that pretty much sealed it.

Liam probably would never admit it, but sitting at the table as Nina started to clear away plates that were once filled with turkey, stuffing, mashed potatoes and cranberry sauce, Liam felt he made the right choice. The conversation had been light and airy, mostly about Nina's job at the medical center and a school project Bessie was working on that her father promised to help with. Liam made the obligatory offer to help clean-up, but Nina shooed him and Tillman into the living room.

As they got settled into their respective chairs, Tillman with his Budweiser and Liam drinking his Coke, they switched on the TV and began to watch the Detroit Lions take on the New York Jets. They watched in silence for about 10 minutes before Tillman addressed the 800-pound elephant in the room.

"You know, Liam," Tillman said, still watching the game. "Bernstein is going to run that Cocoanut Grove story in the *Globe* next Wednesday."

"I know," Liam answered. He took a sip of his drink. "Nothing I can do about it."

"When it comes out, Conor Fitzroy may be the least of your problems."

"Conor Fitzroy will never be the least of my problems," Liam responded, perhaps a little harsher than he intended. Tillman picked up on it.

"I didn't mean it that way, man."

Liam nodded. "I know; I didn't mean to snap. Sorry."

"It's cool."

"Dinner was great by the way," Liam said.

"Yeah, my lady is a great cook."

Bessie ran into the room carrying a pad of paper and stood beside his chair. "Uncle Liam (Liam wasn't sure when she started calling him that, but he liked the sound of it), look! I drew a picture of you!" She handed it to him. Liam smiled as he looked at the drawing, as only an eight-year old can envision it. The figure in the drawing was wearing a shirt and pants. Bessie had colored the pants red, but one of the legs was colored brown from the knee down. Liam smiled.

"I love it," he said. "It goes right up on the wall in my house!"

Bessie smiled, flashed him a peace sign, and said, "Groovy!" She then ran back to her mother.

Liam looked at Tillman. "Groovy?"

Tillman shrugged. "Guess she picked it up from kids at school."

About an hour later, as Tillman tried to stifle turkey-influenced yawns, Liam said his goodbyes, giving both Nina and Bessic hugs. Tillman walked outside with him. The air was crisp and dry, although there was a prediction of light snow later that evening. Liam turned to look at Tillman.

"Listen," Liam said. "If things go south for me after that story runs, I need you to still carry on and try and nail this bastard before anyone else dies."

"I will."

"Promise me," Liam said in earnest. Tillman stared at Liam and nodded.

"I will."

Liam nodded and patted Tillman on the chest. He nodded once more and walked to his car which was at the end of the block. Tillman watched him leave and suddenly felt incredibly sad.

In a basement apartment on a side street in the South End, a block from Boston City Hospital, Conor Fitzroy was celebrating Thanksgiving in a much different way. A half-eaten grilled cheese sandwich sat on a wooden table alongside a half-empty bottle of Bushmills Irish Whiskey.

Wearing nothing but a dirty bathrobe, Conor looked at his reflection in a dusty wall mirror. Slowly he used his finger to trace the scarring on the left side of his face, marveling for a moment on how the reflection in the mirror gave the illusion it was actually on the *right* side. He thought this amusing, but only for a moment. Then, his thoughts returned to the task at hand, which would be his most glorious achievement, and one that will be talked about for generations to come. He looked at the 11x17 poster taped on the far wall and smiled.

"You can't always get what you want," he said half to himself. "But if you try sometimes you just might find get what you need." With that he laughed out loud and grabbed the Bushmills, downing most of the remainder of the bottle in one large gulp.

Finally, in Charlestown, Nora Bernstein stood behind her husband as he typed away at what he hoped would be the final draft of his Spotlight piece on the Cocoanut Grove. She had her hands on Robbie's neck, kneading out the tension knots she could feel through his shirt. She also knew about his sister and how cathartic this story was for him. They had returned home a few hours before, choosing to enjoy Thanksgiving dinner at the Parker House in Boston. As soon as they returned Robbie went straight to work.

"How's it coming?" she asked.

"Good... I think," he responded. "With this I can tie up two loose strings; who was responsible for the fire that killed Peggy..."

186

"And 460 other people," Nora quickly said, trying to keep her husband focused.

"Of course." He said quickly. "And it ties the Fitzroys to the First National Bank heist the same night; the reason for Liam Mulvaney setting the fire."

"I thought Conor Fitzroy set the fire," Nora said. Robbie stopped typing.

"He did; technically," Robbie said. "But Liam... Liam...." He paused. Nora waited. But Robbie didn't say more. He just went back to his typing. Nora kissed Robbie on the top of the head and decided to leave him to his work. She was happy they had planned to get away this weekend.

Chapter Eighteen

Boston... Tuesday, November 28, 1972

Sitting at his kitchen table on a chilly Tuesday morning, Terry Tillman was concentrating so hard his head was starting to pound. The fires have been consuming the city for nearly six months and all they know at this time it that Conor Fitzroy is the madman and the messages he had sent to Liam all contained lyrics to songs by The Rolling Stones..... *but for what purpose?*

"Terry... *Terry!*"

His wife's voice wrestled him from his thoughts. He looked up and saw her standing beside him with her arms crossed and a frustrated look on her face.

"Hmmm...yeah?"

"You promised Bessie you'd help her with her homework assignment before she heads off to school in a couple of hours."

Tillman looked down and saw his daughter holding a magazine. "I need to cut out pictures for school," she said, holding up a *LIFE* magazine. "I need help with the scissors."

Tillman smiled. "Sure, little bug, sit down and we'll work on it." He watched her drag a chair to the table and crawl up on it. She placed the magazine and scissors on the table.

"So, what do we have to do?"

"The teacher wants us to go to the pages and cut out pictures of … um, *adtisings*… of things that we find in our kitchen, in our bathroom and in our bedroom," she said, turning the big pages.

Tillman knew she meant advertisements but chose not to correct her at this time.

"Then we have to use Elmer's Glue and paste them on pieces of paper," Bessie explained. "And whoever does the best gets a prize!"

"Well, in that case," Tillman said. "We better get started if we want to be the winner!"

Tillman and Bessie worked on the project for a little more than an hour. On the table in front of him were cut-out magazine ads for Swanson Frozen TV Dinners, Velveeta Cheese, Dippity-Do Hair Gel, and the always popular SPAM. Bessie had decided to take a break and go watch cartoons.

Satisfied that he had performed his fatherly duties admirably, Tillman closed the magazine with its tattered pages and looked at the cover. At first it seemed just like any other *LIFE* magazine cover, but then his brain started to process what he was seeing on the table in front of him and his eyes grew wide.

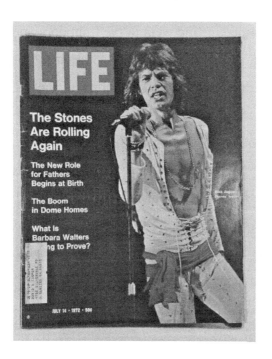

Quickly, Tillman flipped through what was left of the pages until he came to the cover story with its headline: **Stones Kick-Off 34 City U.S. Tour.** He stared at the page for several minutes, and then yelled to his wife who was in the other room.

"Nina! Where's today's *Globe*?"

"Probably still outside," she responded.

Tillman jumped up and went to the front door and grabbed the paper off the stoop. He rummaged through the pages until he found the section he was looking for and took it back to the table. He rifled through the entertainment pages, past movie ads for *Deliverance, Super Fly* and *Last Tango in Paris,* until he came to the fairly small music ads for John Lee Hooker at Paul's Mall, Jonathan Richman at Bunratty's and some group called Aerosmith playing at a college up on the North Shore. But then he turned the page and saw a full-page ad and everything suddenly made sense. He sat back in his chair. "Damn!"

Tillman jumped from his chair, grabbed his jacket and car keys and quickly bolted out the back door. Nina heard the door open and shut and came into the kitchen, only to find her husband gone.

"What the...?" she said to herself. Then she looked at the newspaper on the table and brought her hand to her mouth. "Oh, God!"

LADIES AND GENTLEMEN...

THE ROLLING STONES

AMERICAN TOUR 1972
WITH STEVIE WONDER

BOSTON
GARDEN

Tuesday
Nov. 28th
7:00pm

With the light Tuesday morning traffic Tillman was able to make it from his home in Dorchester to Liam's South Boston apartment in 20 minutes. He pulled into an open spot in front of a green three-decker on P Street, just a block up from the MDC Skating Rink and Castle Island. Turning off the engine, Tillman suddenly felt a twinge of apprehension. As a Negro, travelling around the streets of predominantly white South Boston had put his radar at full attention. When he exited the car he saw a group of three or four young men on the corner of P & 6th Streets standing in front of a variety store looking at him with curiosity, although there didn't seem to be any malice in their intent. Tillman took the steps up to the first floor apartment and rang the bell.

After a few more rings, the door finally opened and Liam, wearing just a bathrobe, looked at him in surprise.

"Tillman... what the hell are you doing here so early?"

"We need to talk."

"It's that important?"

"Would a brother being driving around Southie in daylight if it wasn't?"

Liam sighed and stepped aside. "Well, you better come in before the property values start to drop."

Tillman walked into the living room and looked around. He shook his head. There were clothes everywhere piled on chairs, newspapers and magazines scattered on the coffee table, and at least two empty pizza boxes.

"Damn, Liam."

"Maid's day off," Liam said. "He grabbed a pile of clothes and threw them behind the couch. "Sit. Want a Coke?"

Tillman sat down. "No, I'm good." Liam sat down across from him in a big recliner chair.

"So what's so important?" Liam asked as he started to rummage through a pizza box on the table.

"I think I know what Conor's end game is."

That stopped Liam in his tracks. "What?"

Tillman leaned forward. "It's all tied into the notes he was leaving; the Rolling Stones' songs. The clues... the roadmap you said he called them."

"Okay?"

Tillman looked around. "Is today's paper in this mess somewhere?" Liam leaned over the side of the chair and grabbed the *Boston Globe*. He handed it to Tillman, his curiosity piqued. He watched Tillman quickly sort through the pages until he found the one he wanted. He folded it back and handed it to Liam.

For a few moments Liam just stared at the full-page ad for the concert, but said nothing. Eventually he looked up at Tillman.

"Check the date," Tillman said.

Liam looked back at the ad and Tillman could see his eyes grow wide. "November 28," Liam said softly. "Tonight." He looked back up at Tillman, who was up from the sofa and pacing the room.

"A sold-out show," Tillman said. "What? Maybe 17,000 people?"

Liam let the paper drop on the table. "That psychopath is going to torch the Boston Garden on the 30th anniversary of the Cocoanut Grove fire! *That's* what all the messages were about; all the song lyrics."

Tillman rubbed his hand through his small afro as he sat back down. "What the hell are we going to do? We have to tell the police."

Liam slowly shook his head. "I'm not sure that's the best course of action."

Tillman was stunned. "What, are you nuts?"

Liam placed his hands on his knees. "Hear me out. There haven't been any incidences so far this month, the city is starting to get back to normal, and the mayor isn't going to want to cancel a show like this some 12 hours before it starts. Remember all the protests and riots last summer that he had to put up with? Do you think he wants to go to war with 17,000 angry fans on Causeway Street because the show was cancelled at the last minute?"

Tillman continued to stare at him in disbelief. Liam continued. "We know Conor's plan; I can stop him. I know I can!" Liam clenched the bathrobe draped across his knees with his fists. "*I need to do this, Tillman.* I created Conor Fitzroy 30 years ago when I agreed to open that door. The people who have died this summer; *the people who died 30 years ago;* that's all on me."

Tillman bit his bottom lip as he thought about what Liam had said. "You know when Conor gets arrested—if he gets arrested—all will come out about your part in those deaths 30 years ago."

"Probably doesn't matter; Bernstein's running his *Globe* piece tomorrow anyway," Liam answered. Tillman saw Liam's eye twitch.

"What?"

Liam looked at Tillman. "I just remembered Bernstein said he had tickets to the Stones' concert; his wife's a huge Mick Jagger fan. That's how he knew what the messages meant; that they were song lyrics."

Liam grabbed the phone and dialed as fast as he could. A woman answered.

"*Boston Globe.* How may I direct your call?"

"Robbie Bernstein."

"I'm sorry, Mr. Bernstein is off today."

"Do you have a home number… it's vitally important?"

"I'm sorry, sir. We're not allowed to give out personal information."

Liam's hand gripped the phone tighter. "This is very important; I need to speak with him."

199

"I'm sorry, sir… we have our rules. Besides, I know for a fact he went away for the weekend with his wife. He'll be back in the office tomorrow morning.

Maybe not Liam thought to himself. He hung up without saying goodbye. He looked at Tillman and shook his head.

"What are we going to do?" Tillman asked.

Liam headed for the bedroom. "The first thing I'm going to do is get dressed. What you're going to do is find out how we can get our hands on the architectural plans for the Boston Garden."

In his bedroom Liam heard Tillman leave. When he was sure he was gone he opened the night stand next to his bed and looked down at the .44. This was going to end one way or the other he thought to himself.

Chapter Nineteen

Boston... Tuesday, November 28, 1972

Tillman and Liam sat in Liam's car, parked illegally around the back of the Boston Garden, where the loading area was located. A few bored-looking security guards stood around smoking and stomping their feet to try and keep warm on this late-November evening. It was 8:30 p.m. and thousands of people were still pouring into the concert, at least those who didn't want to hear Stevie Wonder as the opening act. The Stones were scheduled to hit the stage about 9 p.m. and people were already drinking pretty heavily as they strolled towards the Boston Garden. Cars inched their way through the crowded streets blasting the Rolling Stones from car radios and 8-track tapes. Everyone was in a festive mood.

Tillman had found an old blueprint of the Boston Garden from when it was built in 1928 at the Boston Public Library, and they had it opened up on the car's dashboard. Liam traced an area with his finger.

"It makes sense that if Conor is planning something big it's going to happen in the basement area, so he can achieve maximum up-burn." Liam now ran his hand across the sheet. "From what I can see the lower levels have a lot of open space—mostly storage—with several rooms sectioned off."

Using the car's dome light along with a penlight he brought with him, Tillman leaned in a little closer. On the blueprint the storage rooms beneath the main floor were outlined with a thin white line.

"Why does that room look different?" he asked, putting his finger on a room with a *thick* white line, setting it apart from the others. Liam looked at the key to the side of the blueprint and traced his finger down the list. He stopped when he found the one he was looking for. "It's called a... 'high level storage' room."

"Which means what?"

Liam shrugged. "Don't know; but I guess we'll find out." He folded up the blueprint as small as he could and shoved it into his pants pocket. "Let's get going."

"Do you think he's in there?" Tillman asked as he opened the car door.

"I'd bet my life on it."

* * * * *

It's a good thing Terry Tillman didn't take that bet because he would have lost.

Several hours earlier Conor, now disguised as a delivery person with fake credentials, had pulled his pickup truck up to a loading dock and off-loaded an industrial size laundry cart, approximately 47 inches long, 32 inches wide, and at least three-feet deep. The top of the cart was covered in a tarp and a security guard who was more interested in his crossword puzzle than Conor, waved him through. If that guard had shown more interest in the cart's contents instead of a six-letter word for a hand tool, he would have been both surprised and confused to see it full of movie film. And not just any movies, but the classics; *Gone With The Wind, Citizen Kane, The Man Who Knew Too Much* and, Conor's personal favorite, *Casablanca*. But then again, if the guard was that curious, Conor likely would have slit his throat.

Having access to the same blueprints that Tillman and Liam had, Conor also knew there was another room beneath the Garden's floor, but unlike Tillman and Liam he knew what it was designed for. The room was encased in lead and is used to store highly-flammable materials. Although the Boston Garden had no air-conditioning, this one room was designed with a small cooling unit. It was the perfect place for Conor to store the highly-volatile laundry hamper and its combustible contents until show time.

Conor sat on a stool beneath the stage area and he could feel the beat of the music and the roar of the crowd. In some ways he was saddened by what was about to happen; he had some fond memories of the old place. When he was almost 10 his da took him to see the Bruins play the Chicago Blackhawks. The

Bruins beat them handedly with Dit Clapper scoring two goals. And in 1940 he had ringside seats to watch Joe Louis pummel Al McCoy in six rounds. Good times; long ago.

His plan was beautiful in its simplicity. Reaching into his pocket he took out The Rolling Stones set-list for the upcoming show, an easy $50 bribe to the sound engineer accomplished this nicely. He looked at it:

Brown Sugar
Bitch
Rocks Off
Gimme Shelter
Happy
Tumbling Dice
Love in Vain
Sweet Virginia
You Can't Always Get What You Want
All Down the Line
Midnight Rambler
Bye Bye Johnny
Rip This Joint
Jumpin' Jack Flash
Street Fighting Man

Hmmm, he thought to himself, good show; lots of classic songs. Mick and the boys were set to take the stage at 9 p.m.

Conor would let the band plow through the first couple of songs, just to get the crowd more pumped up, and when he heard Keith Richards' classic opening chords on "Gimme Shelter" it would be show time down below.

Now, what many people didn't know is that the Boston Garden put in a hydraulic lift years back that goes from the basement level up to a hole in the stage. When this happens, a part of the stage slides open and the void is filled with the platform from below rising up into place. It had been used by many performers to make the maximum grand entrance. It looks pretty cool when it actually happens Conor had to admit, having seen a magician do something similar at a show in London.

Why is this important? Simply because it is the mechanism from which Conor Fitzroy will create the ultimate finale. While 17,000 fans are singing along to "Gimme Shelter," Conor's plan is to wheel the laundry cart full of film the 30 or so feet from the protective room and onto the hydraulic lift. Push a button on the controls, and in a less than a minute a very surprised Mick Jagger will wonder why a laundry cart has suddenly appeared on stage in the middle of his song.

It's also important to remember that light also emits heat, and sometimes a lot of it. just stand a few feet from any living room lamp after taking the shade off and you will definitely feel noticeable heat. So it's understandable that stage lighting is especially prone to getting very hot and emitting extremely high degrees of heat. In his twisted mind, Conor could close his eyes and see the brutally hot stage lights hit the nitrate film, setting off a mini A-bomb and turning a good portion of the sold-out Boston Garden crowd—and five middle-aged rockers—into pretty much just ash and bone while he sat protected in the lead-lined room below.

* * * * *

Ten minutes before the band was ready to hit the stage, Liam and Tillman, using their fire investigator credentials, easily gained access to the inside of the Boston Garden. In order to get to the area that leads beneath the stage they would have to cut through part of the concourse where the refreshments are sold.

* * * * *

Sitting in their seats in Loge 43 just to the left of the stage, Robbie Bernstein and his wife, Nora, were eagerly anticipating the band's arrival, having thoroughly enjoyed Stevie Wonder's 60-minute set. Robbie and Nora agreed they still had a few minutes for Robbie to head out and grab two more beers. As Robbie made his way out to the concourse did a double-take as he saw both Liam Mulvaney and Terry Tillman flash their badges at a security guard and go down an opening where a sign was clearly posted "Authorized Personnel Only." Robbie thought to himself, *"What the hell...?"* But then his reporter instincts took over and he followed them through the opening (his *Boston Globe* press pass did the trick), quietly going down the same ramp.

* * * * *

Listening closely from inside the protective room, Conor could hear the Rolling Stones being introduced as the crowd noise level increased dramatically, wisps of dust now falling from the ceiling above his head. Smiling, he pushed the cart out of the room to get it into position, but the smile faded when he pushed the cart just a few feet out of the room and then saw

208

Liam and Tillman standing in front of him. Liam was holding a gun.

"It's over Conor," Liam said. But he was surprised when Conor didn't seem the least bit fazed. He simply pulled the tarp off the laundry cart and both Liam and Tillman gasped and took an involuntary step backwards when they saw the cart was filled to the very top with film.

Standing behind the cart, Conor gave a grim smile. "Now, boyo, I wouldn't think about shooting that gun around here," he said, holding up a strand of film. "So how about you walk that gun over here and I'll just hold on to it for safe keeping."

Liam wasn't sure what to do. He looked at the sign above the door that Conor had just walked out of and it all became clear to him; at least he hoped it was. But he had to take the gamble. He looked at Tillman… and winked. His partner was confused by the gesture. Then Liam started to walk slowly towards Conor and the cart. Conor's smile broadened as he held out his hand; he loved winning. When he was only a few feet from the cart, and mustering all the momentum he could even with one leg,

Liam bolted forward and pushed the cart into a surprised Conor, who suddenly felt himself backpedaling into the protected room, his mouth open in surprise as he fell backwards, the contents of the overturned cart covering him as he sat on the floor. Liam tossed the cart aside and looked down at Conor, who was trying to separate himself from the film strips that covered him like slithering brown snakes. Liam then quickly slammed the door shut behind him and locked it.

Outside Tillman pounded on the metal door. "Liam, open up!" he shouted, hitting the door even harder with his fists. "God damn you!"

Robbie came up behind him, totally confused as to what was unfolding. "What the hell is going on?" he asked. He looked around. "Where's Mulvaney?"

Tillman turned to face him. "He locked himself in this room with Conor Fitzroy."

Robbie was still confused. "Why would he do that?"

"Because Conor Fitzroy has enough nitrate film to turn the Boston Garden into a mini-Hiroshima."

Robbie turned pale. "Oh my God!"

"I think Liam figures a lead-lined room will contain the blast."

Robbie found it hard to form his next words. "And if it doesn't?"

Conor sat amidst the film, angrily glaring at Liam. "So what now, you think you stopped me? You think I don't have other plans?" He let out a snort. "Big deal. I get arrested for what; trespassing with some dangerous materials? I'll be out in a few years. But you, boyo, you'll likely still be in prison when I tell the world what you did as a lad. All the people who are dead simply for a $100." Conor laughed again.

Liam didn't join in the laughter, but he did have a small smile on his face. "You know, Conor, I haven't had a good night's sleep in 30 years," he said, putting the gun down on the floor. "I close my eyes and I see sheets covering bodies on a sidewalk. I see ghosts and ghostly things." He reached into his pants pocket and Conor blanched when he saw what Liam was holding in his hand. "But you know something, Conor," Liam asked serenely, holding up the object. "I think I might finally get some rest now." And with that he spun the wheel on the cigarette lighter and watched for a second as it ignited. "Good night, Conor," Liam said. "Say hello to Fitzsy in hell." And with that he tossed the lighter on to the film covering Conor, who screamed *"NO-O-O-O-O!!"* A second later the room exploded into flame, light and death.

Tillman, who was leaning against the thick metal door was jolted by the tremor from the explosion within, which actually buckled parts of the door. Robbie struggled to regain his balance. Both men looked at each other. With the realization of what just happened, Tillman slid down on to the seat of his pants, his back, even with a jacket on, feeling the warmth from the door. He put his head in his hands and sobbed.

Robbie knelt down beside Tillman and touched his arm. "I'm sorry," he said. Tillman looked up at him, tears running down his cheeks. He shrugged. "It doesn't matter, does it?" Tillman said, wiping an eye with his sleeve. "Once your story hits tomorrow, that's all the world is going to remember about Liam Mulvaney."

Robbie stood up and looked down at Tillman. "Maybe not," was all he said as he turned and went back to his wife.

With 17,000 people yelling, screaming and stomping their feet, no one at the concert had even an inkling of how close they had come to disaster. Nora Bernstein sat in her seat listening to the Stones rip through a scorching rendition of "Rocks Off" and wondered why it was taking her husband so long to buy two beers.

Epilogue

Boston... Tuesday, November 28, 1992

It was just after 3 p.m. and most of the onlookers, press and dignitaries had long departed Piedmont Street in Boston's Bay Village. They had all gathered for a ceremony commemorating the 50th anniversary of the 1942 Cocoanut Grove fire. A modest, bronze plaque was placed in the sidewalk at 17 Piedmont Street, near where the revolving door stood that took the lives of 40 people trying to escape the fire and smoke. There were 492 deaths overall.

The plaque was created by Tony Marra, the youngest survivor of the Cocoanut Grove fire. Tony was a 15-year-old busboy when he cheated death. They embedded the plaque in the sidewalk with considerable reverence, and several politicians, among them Mayor Ray Flynn and City Councilors Bruce Bolling and Albert "Dapper" O'Neil, paid their due respects. They then posed for the prerequisite photos.

The plaque read: "As a result of this terrible tragedy, major changes were made in the fire codes and improvements in the treatment of burn victims, not only in Boston but across the nation."

A lone figure stood over the plaque, a slim man with his head bowed; the collar of his overcoat turned up to ward off the November breeze. He holds two long-stem roses in his hand. A black man approaches to the side of him, his hands deep in his coat pockets. A beautiful young woman has her arm interlocked through his. The slim figure looks at the man and woman and smiles.

"Mr. Tillman," he says.

"Mr. Bernstein," the man answers. "Robbie, this is my daughter, Bessie. She's attending BU; getting her Masters in Journalism."

That made Robbie smile. "I wish you the best of luck, my dear," he said sincerely.

"Thank you," she replied, and then she kissed her father on the cheek. "I'll be in the car with mom. Take your time."

"Okay, hon." She gives Robbie a small smile and walks off.

"Beautiful girl," Robbie said, looking at the plaque.

"Thanks. I wondered what happened to you after that night," Tillman said. "You just kind of... disappeared. I never got to say thanks for not including Liam in the story."

Robbie let out a sigh. "It was an easy fix. As far as the world knows Conor Fitzroy entered the club thanks to some *unidentified* employee opening the back door. At least that was Carl Lumley's story.

"Where *did* you go?"

"*The Baltimore Sun*," Robbie replied. "But I had to come back for this." Both men looked down at the sidewalk in silence.

"I'm sorry about your sister," Tillman finally said. Robbie nodded his thanks.

"Liam saved my life that night at the Boston Garden," Robbie said. "And he saved my wife's life. Hell, how many other lives did he save?" He looked down at the sidewalk. "I'd say Liam Mulvaney has wiped out the red in his ledger."

Tillman put a hand on Robbie's shoulder and gave him a small squeeze. He then turned and walked to his car, leaving Robbie alone with his thoughts. Robbie knelt down and laid a single rose on the plaque. "I miss you, big sister." He then placed the other rose beside it. Standing back up, he took one last look and then buttoned the top button of his coat, turned, and walked away.

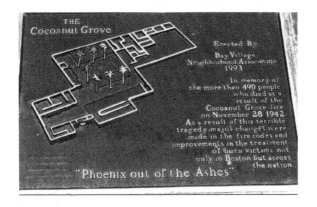

Justice

Will troubled mind shake off a guilty past,

Or will it burn in ever endless pain?

Shall peace be found for murdered souls at last,

Or will justice fail, truth obscure remain?

Notes of madness trace arson's flaming path,

Under dark of night, insane murder stalks;

Citizenry alarmed, snarls in fear and wrath;

Doors strongly barred, secured with double locks!

Suffering soul, the loss, years since Forty-Two,

Of five-hundred slain, (one with hair of red),

Vows with heavy heart, follow every clue;

In each waking hour, justice for the dead!

Ashes in the wind, voices in the breeze,

Bones seared and blackened, tragic memories.

-- Frank X. Roberts

Coming in Summer 2023

Be notified of this and all upcoming releases. Follow the author at

Amazon.com: Stephen A. White: books, biography, latest update

January 10, 2023 – March 22, 2023

Made in the USA
Middletown, DE
22 August 2023

37090636R00126